H.N. WAKE

SECRETS OF THE ANGELS

Vinci Books

vinci-books.com

Published by Vinci Books Ltd in 2025

1

Copyright © H.N. Wake 2021

The author has asserted their moral right to be identified as the author of this work in accordance with the Copyright, Designs and Patents Act 1988. This work is a work of fiction. Names, characters, places and incidents are the product of the author's imagination or are used fictitiously. Any resemblance to actual persons, living or dead, places and incidents is entirely coincidental.
All rights reserved. No part of this publication may be copied, reproduced, distributed, stored in any retrieval system, or transmitted in any form or by any means, including photocopying, recording, or other electronic or mechanical methods, nor used as a source for any form of machine learning including AI datasets, without the prior written permission of the publisher.
The publisher and the author have made every effort to obtain permissions for any third party material used in this book and to comply with copyright law. Any queries in this respect should be brought to the attention of the publisher and any omissions will be corrected in future editions.
A CIP catalogue record for this book is available from the British Library.
Paperback ISBN: 9781036704858
The EU GPSR authorised representative is Logos Europe, 9 rue Nicolas Poussion, 17000 La Rochelle, France contact@logoseurope.eu

By H.N. Wake

FBI Agent Domini Walker

Sound of a Furious Sky
Hidden in the Silence
Secrets of the Angels
Echoes of Thunder

Prologue

The telephone shrilled twice.

On socked feet, Dom Walker rushed into the kitchen and grabbed the shiny, yellow handset. "Walkers."

An older man with a raspy voice asked, "Esther Walker?"

It was the gravity of his tone that made her glance into the living room. Sitting in a bright sun patch on the red velvet couch, her mother, Esther, held a cup of tea and stared at the wall above the television. She wasn't watching the show on the television. She almost never watched the actual programs.

Dom lied, "Yes."

"This is Precinct 9."

Her heart thumped. "Yes?"

"There's been an arrest."

That must be what had kept their father, NYPD Officer Stewart Walker, late. He must be processing a criminal. Relieved, she breathed deeply. "Ah, ok."

The hoarse voice said, "Uh, no, ma'am. It's not like that."

From the back room, her young brother, Beecher, hollered, "Is it Dad?"

"Ma'am, I'm afraid to tell you that your husband has been arrested. Officer Walker has been booked into jail."

Dom blinked.

"I'm sorry to be the messenger, but this is just a courtesy call. I expect he'll be calling you soon. I advise you to stay by the phone."

"Yes."

"Goodbye." The phone line went dead.

In her ear, the dial tone buzzed. The large handset felt cold as she gently set it back on the hook. The long-curled cord swung against the kitchen wall.

Goodbye is a funny word. What is good about ending the conversation?

Just last night, her father had kissed her forehead as he had done for fifteen years. "I'll bring home donuts. Tell Beecher we can watch cartoons in the morning." And off he'd gone.

Dom turned toward the sun patch.

Esther took a sip of tea.

Beecher hollered, "Is that Dad? Is he coming?"

The phone warbled again.

She snatched the handset.

Her father, Stewart, said, "Dom?"

Her voice cracked. "Dad?"

"Hi, honey. Yes. It's me." He sounded calm.

Her heart raced. "Are you in jail?"

"It's a big mistake. It's going to be fine."

"Dad?"

"It's going to be fine. I am fairly sure I know what happened. There's been a mistake and I'm going to fix it."

"Dad—"

"My Dom, listen to me very carefully. This may take a few days to sort out. There is going to be stuff in the newspapers and on television. There may even be reporters that come to the apartment. I need you to look out for Beecher. You two have to stick together."

"Dad—"

"Don't talk to anyone. Just ignore it all. I'm going to sort it out. I promise. If they need your mother, you get Aunt Lucille to accompany her. Don't let your mother do anything on her own."

She understood. Her mother wasn't capable of handling the grocery store, let alone her husband in jail.

"You stay away from all this. You just focus on taking care of Beecher and staying away from all this mess."

Her voice squeaked. "Dad?"

"You are going to be fine, sweetheart." His voice was gentle. His voice was always gentle. "You are smart. And strong. You've always been strong."

That was the last thing he ever said to her.

Part I

Secrets
infesting my half-sleep…
did you enter my wound from another wound
brushing mine in a crowd…

—Lola Ridge, "Secrets"

Chapter One

Dom Walker had been awake for twenty minutes watching the sunrise chase the shadows from the room. During their teen years, she and Beecher hadn't known to buy curtains. When Beecher went to college, she had gotten him cheap white curtains similar to the ones in the other dorm rooms. Later, he had taken those silly curtains into the city. When he moved back into her house, they had gotten nicer ones. But she noticed that, like her, he never drew them closed. She suspected he also preferred to see the sky. Childhood habits were hard to shake.

The guest room had new curtains. Sensitive to the new living situation, Dom had wanted Mila Pascale to feel as welcome and safe as possible, so she'd gone to a high-end store and purchased an expensive set. They must have worked, because Mila had been with them for six months.

She stretched her legs into the cold region of the sheets and pointed her toes. A mild shock rippled through her right foot. The physical therapist cautioned that toes, always in use, rarely healed smoothly or quickly. Dom would have a few more weeks of mild pain.

Next to her, Tinks the Tongue stretched into full-body extension. Tiny paws dug into her arm.

From the kitchen, water ran in the sink.

Beecher was up.

The full house had settled into a harmonious morning routine. Beecher woke at six a.m. and would put on the coffee. Tinks was second to the kitchen to ensure her breakfast. Mila followed a few minutes later and would walk Tinks around the block as Beecher got breakfast ready. Dom was last. They sipped their coffee silently at the kitchen table while reading their chosen news outlets. On the days that Beecher taught at City College, he would head out before eight. Mila always left the house twelve minutes before ten for the train to NYU. You could set your clock by that girl's movements.

Dom was the only one without a morning routine. Investigations made that impossible.

The refrigerator door opened and Tinks poked her head out from under the sheet.

Dom whispered, "Go ahead."

The Chihuahua scurried over the pillow and jumped off the bed. Toenails tapped down the hall.

The twang of coffee tickled Dom's nose. She rolled on her side and gazed out the window. Beyond, the sky was a cheerful blue as if to welcome a nice easy day between cases.

The back door banged open.

Dom held her breath.

A woman's deep voice boomed, "Beecher Walker, it borders on sinful for you to look so heavenly this early in the morning. You are a divine sight for tired eyes."

Beecher laughed. "Lea Peck."

"The smell of that caffeine is an absolute aphrodisiac."

Beecher said, "It'll be ready in two minutes."

FBI Staff Operations Specialist Lea Peck was here on a Saturday morning. Unannounced.

Dom sat up, rolled off the bed, and grabbed a sweatshirt.

Sitting at the table, Lea Peck rolled her eyes upwards and savored another sip of coffee. "Amen."

Lea had worked with Dom over the last three years. She was the sharp, sassy product of a Baptist pastor father, an English teacher mother, and a small southern town. Her verbal embellishments were equal parts Biblical references and bold swear words. Her mind was as quick as a computer. She was the ideal research support.

Dom sat opposite Lea as Beecher settled at the head of the table.

Lea set her mug down. "How is everything this fine morning?"

From the hallway, Mila shuffled into the room. Her big black eyes took in the scene as she poured herself a cup of coffee, sat in the remaining chair, and waved Tinks into her lap.

Lea looked to Dom. "I'm here for a reason."

Dom said, "We gathered that."

"Well, I've got something to tell y'all."

This was unusual. "You don't want to do this in the office?"

"It's actually for all of y'all." Lea raised her palms. "It's not going to be life changing, but small can be powerful."

Three sets of eyes watched her.

"It's about Dartanian Velk."

All three leaned back.

Dom and Beecher's father, Stewart Walker, had been an NYPD officer until he had been caught with four others in a department sting. The Filthy Five had stood trial. Three of the five had been acquitted. Stewart was sentenced to two years. A month into his prison sentence, he committed suicide. Not long after, their mother Esther had abandoned them. The family guilt was never far from Beecher and Dom, like the storm on the horizon of a perfect summer day.

Last month, in a stunning series of events, Esther arrived in New York and announced that she had received a drunken confession letter from the wife of one of the Filthy Five. Stewart had been set up.

Earlier, Mila had taken it upon herself to research the Filthy Five and had uncovered a tenuous reference to Dartanian Velk, the NYPD Head of Internal Affairs at the time of the Filthy Five. In the shocking meeting last month, Esther had recognized the name.

Lea said, "We acknowledge that the Velk thread is super interesting, right?"

Beecher shrugged. "Esther isn't exactly a reliable source. Just because she remembers Velk, doesn't mean he had anything to do with it. And a drunken confession isn't exactly state's evidence."

"Yes, but as NYPD Head of Internal Affairs, Velk surely would have known about the sting."

Dom's jaw tightened. Stewart's death, coupled with Esther's mental illness, had precipitated their childhood abandonment. She wasn't prepared to open the Stewart Walker wounds, despite the possibilities of the new revelations.

Lea turned to her. "Dom, I know you said we'd wait. That you wanted to sit on this new intel. But I was finishing up a shift last night at around 2 a.m. and as I was sitting at the screen, I thought, why not sniff around. When I get going, I get going. And boy, is Velk interesting. So, he was here in New York as Head of Internal Affairs for six years. From 1997 to 2003. He's the top IA guy in the greatest city in the world. Crazy authority. Insane career. In short, he's at his peak. But then he moves to Philly to head up their IA. Who moves from New York to Philly? By any measure that's a demotion." Lea held up a finger. "I haven't actually answered that first question. But regardless, he then puts in five years in Philly."

Everyone took a sip of coffee.

Lea continued. "Now, this is where it gets really interesting. After five years, in 2008 he heads out to LA. Head of Internal Affairs LAPD. Nice move. West coast. Sunshine. Beaches. I'd take it, too, if New York weren't the fucking crown jewel. Which it is. But why all the moving? Seems weird, no? Maybe he's trying to run from something?"

She was met with blank faces.

"Ok, don't go there with me. That's fine. I spent enough time trying to figure it out and didn't find anything. I get your hesitancy." She waffled her hand in the air. "So, I changed tact. And get this: Velk moved to LA and gets himself a house in Brentwood."

More blank stares.

Lea held two hands out wide. "*Brentwood*."

Beecher said, "I'm not following."

"O.J. Simpson, Nicole Brown? That Brentwood?"

Silence.

"Jennifer Garner and Ben Affleck? Tom Brady and Giselle?"

More silence.

Lea placed her hands on the table like a teacher finding

patience with a slow class. "Have none of you ever had aspirations to be a celebrity sports star, making bank, in the mags, walking the red carpet with a hot model? You know, with all the accoutrements that come with wealth? The mountain view infinity pool, the tinted Range Rover, the automatic gate, the live-in cook that makes Oprah's low-carb fried chicken?"

All three shook their heads.

Lea threw her hands up in defeat. "Ok, I can't with you people. Just know that Brentwood is some of the most valuable real estate in all of the United States and our man Velk is currently living much larger than law enforcement salary should allow."

Mila stroked Tinks head. "You were up all night on this?"

Lea pointed at Mila. "Listen, little miss, you never can tell where a lead will take you."

Beecher cleared his throat softly. "I mean, it *may* be something."

Lea snorted. "Hello, hot stuff. Not all investigations start with a smoking gun. They often start with a lil ole theory that you look to prove or disprove." She turned to Dom. "Am I right?"

Dom pushed back from the table, stood and took off at a slow pace around the kitchen. Esther's lead to Velk was worth exploring. But were they going to open that research now? Was it time to dig in?

She leaned on the edge of the sink. The possibility of her father's innocence was breathtaking. What if their research led to a dead end? Or even worse, what if they discovered Stewart Walker had been guilty as charged? Were they prepared to accept that finding? Would Beecher be ok? Would she?

She stared into the drain. Wasn't it better to know one way or the other? Sooner or later, they would have to get to the bottom of his guilt or innocence.

She gripped the edge of the sink. Their research would be unsanctioned. Further, it would be based on the personal vendetta of an FBI Special Agent over her dead father. And it potentially involved one of the most senior law enforcement officers in the country. This was dangerous, dangerous territory. This was job risking territory.

She glanced out the window. Not a single cloud was in the sky.

She turned.

All eyes were on her.

She nodded her head. "Yes. It's time. Let's do this."

Chapter Two

The crowd in Washington Square Park at midmorning was mostly students and dog walkers. By the fountain, a busker was singing James Taylor and a young woman spun a hula-hoop around her waist. Mila Pascale leaned over the fence of the small dog park to watch a chunky pug vainly chase a white terrier. From behind, a small group of students lounging on a blanket laughed loudly at a joke.

Social occasions weren't Mila's thing. Or friends, really. She didn't have the same needs as most for interpersonal interaction or communication. Alone time, lots of alone time, was perfectly fine. It didn't make her sad or happy. It was just the way it was. This singularity allowed her to concentrate for hours, to perform repetitive actions for extended periods, and to fixate on an issue until it was resolved. This was especially true when she was researching grave issues. These traits made her a good researcher and would one day make her invaluable to the FBI.

She pushed off the fence and weaved through oncoming pedestrian traffic toward the southwest corner.

Early that morning, after Lea Peck had left, Dom had looked at her across the kitchen table. "You need to stay away from this."

Mila had stared back.

Dom had pointed a finger at her. "Away."

"Didn't I help discover that the three acquitted members of the Filthy Five were back working at Precinct 9?"

"And I'm thankful for that. You're an excellent researcher and you do great work. But—"

"I need the practice if I'm going to get into Quantico."

Dom shook her head. "You are not getting involved on this one."

"How could it be bad to help you and Beecher and Lea?"

Dom raised her eyebrows. "Seriously?"

Days after Mila discovered the acquitted members of the Filthy Five had regrouped, she had done something super stupid: she'd alerted the Precinct 9 Chief. At the time, it felt like her civic duty. In hindsight, she should have used a more protected, anonymous email. As a result of her missive, two of the officers—monster Robert Gessen and henchman Art Dyson—had chased her from her apartment in the middle of the night and terrorized her in the park. Wolves chasing a lone lamb. After that terrifying night, Dom and Beecher had taken her in. She'd been safe and sound here ever since.

Mila shrugged. "It was a lesson learned."

"Oh, I see. How easy we forget. You can just shrug it off now?"

Mila scowled. "A hard lesson. But learned."

Dom pressed. "It was terrible and not to be repeated. I've got eyes on Gessen and Dyson. That being said, there is absolutely no reason for you to get involved in this. It's too close to home. Literally."

Mila could never repay them. But she could try to. "Maybe I can do some tangentially-related research."

Dom set down her mug. "Mila, I need to not worry about you—"

"But I'm the one that also cracked the Velk connection."

"If I'm going to start working on this, I can't have you getting in trouble again. You understand that, right? I've got this. Why don't you focus on school for now?"

"What if you need an extra set of eyes?"

"There is no urgency. This is a cold case with lots of rabbit holes. I have a feeling we'll be working on it for a while. Probably a year or more—"

"I'm sure there are angles I can pursue that aren't Filthy Five related. Digressive. Extraneous."

"I know what tangential means."

"But I won't do any research on the actual Filthy Five."

Dom sighed. "Why do I have a feeling you're going to ignore me?"

Mila watched her.

Dom crossed her arms. "I can't lock you up in your room."

Mila's face was blank.

"You can be a tough cookie, you know that?"

It was true. She was a tough cookie. She'd seen a lot, been through a lot.

Dom finally shook her head. "Ok, but promise me this, if you go digging, you stay away from the Filthy Five and you tell me or Lea right away if you hit something solid. Deal?"

"Yes."

"I know a lot of things about you now, Mila Pascale.

One thing I know for sure is that you stand by your word. You've just made a promise to me."

Mila had nodded. "I did."

"Ok." Dom had stood. "In the meantime, don't you have homework or studying or something to do?"

Exiting the park, Mila stepped into the corner pizza shop. It was part of her daily ritual. Step one: order pepperoni extra crispy. Step two: ask that they understood extra crispy meant just long enough to burn the ends. Step three: pay. Step four: refuse the glass shaker bottle and ask for a baggie side of Parmesan. Too many people touch the shaker. Too many germs. Step five: accept pizza on paper plate with four napkins. Step six: step outside to eat in peace. No matter what the weather.

For Mila Pascale, orderliness kept the demons at bay and smoothed the memories of Jimmy's bright blue eyes and rabbit tooth grin.

Standing on the corner, she took her first bite. She counted each chew. One. Two. Three. On her third bite, she felt a ghost press against her left side.

She stilled and blinked to silence the bustle of the crowd and the swoosh of a taxi.

Along her body, she could almost feel the tender press of Jimmy's skinny body like the faint spray off a big wave.

She swallowed and glanced down.

There was only empty sidewalk.

She blinked against the sting of tears.

Slowly, she raised her eyes and focused on the scene around her. One. Two. Three.

Her mind cleared.

She took another bite, but the pizza now tasted like sawdust.

She dropped the slice in the wastebasket and stepped from the curb.

She had grave issues to research.

Chapter Three

Fifth Street between Avenue A and B would have looked a lot different in 1999 and the building outside her passenger window—512 Fifth Street—would have had broken windows and trash on the stoop. Inside, the walls would have been thin enough to hear crying babies and loud fights. There may have been intermittent heat. Some of the buildings on this street would have been drug houses or brothels. But East Village had been gentrified over the years and was now home to students, young professionals, and good restaurants. 512 had a slick black door, a video intercom system, and a freshly painted trashcan shed.

Dom looked through the window of the Lancia Fulvia Coupé and sipped her third coffee of the morning. The car had been Stewart Walker's singular treasure. When she was only eight, he had started taking her to the local track. Before each race, with the old passenger seat belt twisted around her, he would drive her through the turns, explaining how to expand the radius of the corner and to hit it wide-tight-wide. Later, she would sit in a folding chair by the pit, eating hot dogs and listening to the banter of the other drivers.

This was the first time Dom had visited the scene of the Filthy Five sting. As a teen, she had done everything within her power to avoid thinking about the case. She had sprinted from the journalists outside their Brooklyn home, had studiously avoided reading or watching the media coverage of the court case, and had stoically ignored the barbs of the high school bullies.

Over the years, she had reviewed the trial transcripts and had often envisioned the actions that had gone down at 512 on that night in 1999.

Before their shift, at 9 p.m., NYPD Officers Robert Gessen and Art Dyson had gone to a local Mexican restaurant for tacos. Gessen was a ten-year veteran of the force with a wife and a young baby at home. His personnel file had four write-ups for misconduct. Dyson was a single guy who liked weightlifting and baseball. For two years, Gessen and Dyson had worked night shifts together. They knew the nuances of the neighborhood.

At 9:30 p.m., they attended the Precinct 9 roll call with Officers Mike Turner and John Belafonte, each fifteen-year veterans of the Precinct.

At 10:08, Gessen and Dyson cruised the southern end of the precinct in a police car.

Turner and Belafonte started their cruise at 10:26.

At 11:26, a call reported shots fired in or around 512 Fifth Street.

Gessen and Dyson responded and arrived at the scene at 11:37.

At 11:52, Gessen and Dyson reported additional shots fired.

Turner and Belafonte responded that they were en route. Three minutes later, they pulled alongside the cruiser.

At 12:03, the precinct chief asked Officer Stewart Walker, assigned to a plainclothes foot patrol shift, to also respond.

At 12:10, Gessen instructed Turner and Belafonte to cover the back alley of the building.

Walker had arrived at the front of the building at 12:20.

Dom set down her coffee and stretched from the car. She walked slowly to the end of the block while she counted the buildings and cornered into the rear alley. A new wooden fence separated the alley from the green trees of a park.

Striding down the alley, she counted down from the corner.

On that fateful night, having reached this rear location, Turner had kicked a hole in the flimsy door and pushed through. He and Belafonte entered the quiet building with guns drawn and moved quickly to open the front door.

At 12:38, Gessen and Dyson rushed in to join them.

Belafonte returned to the rear exit.

Walker remained outside on the stoop.

Officers Gessen, Dyson and Turner—in that order—took the stairs at a rush.

Cornering onto the second-floor landing, Gessen hissed at an old woman to close her door.

Reaching the third floor, the resident in the front apartment pointed them to the closed door of the rear apartment.

With a powerful kick, Gessen sent the rear apartment door flying open.

Dyson was the first officer into the apartment, followed by Turner and Gessen.

The apartment was empty. A single back window was open. Two duffel bags of dollar bills, bricks of cocaine, and handguns had been left on the floor.

Sticking his head out the window, Gessen confirmed that the fire escape was empty, then yelled down to Belafonte.

That night, none of the officers reported having seen any suspects.

Dom reached the shiny black gated rear door for 512 and gazed up three floors.

According to the court testimony of Gessen, Dyson, and Turner, Walker said he knew of an empty warehouse not far from the scene where they could stash the loot. Walker offered to keep an eye on it since he was ending his shift. According to the three officers, Walker had convinced them by saying, "Repay the sacrifice."

At 10 a.m. the next day, the four officers rendezvoused with Walker at the warehouse. They swore an oath not to buy boats or cars or diamonds. They would hide the banknotes in their homes and slowly transfer, with deposits of $999 each, the cash into their accounts.

When the SWAT team had descended, two hours later, the five had been heavily drunk and were easily rounded up.

As Dom turned back to the entrance of the alley, she was hit with a memory of her six-year-old self in Prospect Park.

Leaning over the bike handlebars, her fingers crushed the squishy foam.

Near her ear, Stewart Walker had said, "Tell me the obstacles you see between here and the finish line." His voice was kind, gentle.

"That German Shepherd. The lady with the stroller. That guy sitting on the bench. That baseball."

"Excellent. The baseball will only take a small correction. Now tell me the lines to the finish."

She imagined the course corrections to hit the final curve at top speed. "Close in on dog, keep on my left."

"Excellent. When do you brake?"

"Before the dog, peddle past the dog."

"Agree with that, my girl. Then what?"

"Middle of the path, past the stroller."

"Perfect. Then?"

"Brake near the man's feet."

"Excellent. Great lines. When's your last brake?"

"There, by the guy on the bench."

"What if he stands up?"

She hadn't thought of that. The guy could stand up. Exacerbated, she pulled her hands off the handles. "I don't know."

"Take a second, imagine it happening. What if he stands up and takes a step into the middle of the sidewalk?"

If the guy stood up, her lines were messed up. "I'm screwed."

He chuckled. "Ok, strong language for a kid, but yes, if he stands up, you have to swerve to avoid the baseball. You're in the grass. Your run is over."

"Is he gonna stand up?"

"We don't know."

"Maybe I should wait."

"Nah, a good run is worth taking when you see it."

She grasped the handlebars and leaned out over the wheel.

In her ear, Stewart Walker whispered, "Go!"

Chapter Four

Mila had chosen a quiet stack on the second floor of the massive NYU Bobst Library. Bookshelves towered over the lone desk. On Saturdays, most students were out in the park, which meant the library would remain relatively quiet until lunch. No gum chewing, no whispers, no cracking knuckles. All good.

Under a bright fluorescent light, she slid the plastic chair under the desk, slipped out her laptop, and logged onto the library network. She would start with ordinary internet searches and if she found something from a local newspaper, she'd switch over to the library sources. Her fingers typed *Filthy Five*. As she had promised Dom, she wouldn't dig into this particular angle, but she did want to make sure she hadn't missed anything obvious on Velk.

The first hit was a Village Voice article titled, *Dirty Cops Rounded up in a Sting Operation.* She hesitated before clicking it open.

Stewart Walker, in dress blues with a big gold badge on his right chest, smiled from an official police photo. Dom rarely spoke about her father, but Mila gathered that Stewart had been a kind and attentive man. Next to Walker, the monster Gessen stared at her with beady blue eyes. His short cut blond hair made him look like a Nazi officer. Her jaw tensed. There were nights she woke up in a sweat wondering what he and Dyson would have done if they had captured her in the park.

She straightened her shoulders and puffed her chest. *When I'm an FBI Special Agent, I'm coming for you, Gessen.*

She skimmed the article but found nothing new.

The next keyword search for *Dartanian Velk* returned six articles. Only six? On its own, this was an interesting fact. A Head of Internal Affairs for the biggest law enforcement jurisdiction should surely have made more press. Presumably, he would have attended trials, announced findings, or gone to official events. But maybe he liked to stay behind the scenes. Not everybody liked to be in the public.

She read the first article.

LAPD Head of the Internal Affairs Bureau Visits with Police Union Leader
During his first three months on the job as LAPD's Head of Internal Affairs, Dartanian Velk met with the head of the police union. This was the first meeting of the two heavy hitters and it comes on the heels of a notable ouster of a LAPD officer on charges of misconduct including police brutality and witness tampering. The two men have been locked in an internal battle over the firing. Today's meeting was intended to break the impasse.

The photo at the top of the article showed a thin, dark-haired man exiting the LA headquarters building. He looked tall relative to the police officer beside him. The caption read, *Elusive Head of Internal Affairs, Dartanian Velk, leaves for special meeting.*

Elusive. Sounds like Dartanian Velk did indeed like to stay out of the limelight. It piqued Mila's interest. From her bag, she pulled out a new spiral notebook that she'd purchased for this research. She opened to the first clean page and jotted *private*.

The remaining five articles were about his work. He appeared in two photos: the first in a row of spectators in a courtroom and the second on a stage behind the Philadelphia Police Commissioner. Nothing about his personal life appeared in the press.

Elusive indeed. Mila nodded to herself.

She turned to Facebook, but not surprisingly, Dartanian Velk had no profile. She widened the search to the last name Velk. She scrolled down the list of sixteen individual profile faces in round windows, all named Velk, all with New York listed as their residence. She skimmed for birthdays in the 1960s and clicked open Aurélie Velk whose birthday was offered up like a tribute to the data gods: 1966. She had graduated from Colby College in 1988. She was a thin woman with long dark hair and pronounced features—sharp, angular—and mostly unsmiling. She had a very keen resemblance to Dartanian Velk: this had to be his sister. Aurélie Velk had joined Facebook in 2009 and had very few restrictions on her posts. She posted regularly through 2011—mostly photos of friends and some artwork. She hadn't posted about a husband or a child. Either they didn't want to be on social media, or she was single and childless. She had last posted in October of 2011.

Mila shook her head. Facebook was a gold mine for law enforcement.

Mila opened a new search window, typed in *Aurélie Velk*,

and was rewarded with immediate hits. Aurélie Velk was an artist. Several articles noted her work in local art magazines. Mila logged into the NYU network and did a quick scan for the magazines and editions. A March 2001 edition of *Art World* was available in hard copy in the library.

She gathered up her laptop and bag and headed to the elevator. The stacks she needed were at the back of the building on the fourth floor.

Eight minutes later, Mila strolled between two tall shelves in the back wing. From up ahead in an adjoining aisle a couple was fighting in a whisper. As she approached, she cleared her throat and the couple went silent as she passed.

Finding the shelves with the correct location number, she laid her bag on the linoleum floor and pulled a carton from the shelf. She fingered her way through the magazines until she found the March edition of *Art World*, its cover the painting of a bright orange poppy. She sat crossed legged on the cold floor and skimmed the table of contents. Always skim the table of contents. Flipping through pages for the desired article was incredibly inefficient.

The article she wanted was on page 24: *"Velk Resonates"* accompanied by a full-page photo of the dark, angular Aurélie in a gallery.

"Bingo," she whispered.

Dartanian Velk stood to Aurélie's left, his dark eyes on the camera. To Aurélie's right, a similarly dark-haired, tall man stood next to a curvy woman with light brown short hair. The caption read, *Browning Gallery: Artist Aurélie Velk with her brothers Dartanian and Georgius and sister-in-law Naomi Cantor.*

Hi, Georgius and Naomi. What's up with those names?

Mila slipped out her laptop and typed in *Naomi Cantor.*

Two hits. Both in the Philadelphia Inquirer.

Her fingers paused over the keyboard. Philadelphia? Like Dartanian?

She clicked open the first. It was an obituary. The summary read, *Naomi Ellen Cantor, March 2, 2021. Beloved wife of Dartanian Velk. Survived by her husband and siblings. Relatives and friends invited to the funeral.*

Mila sat back. *Velk was a widower?*

Her second thought was immediate and illogical. *Could widowers be bad people?*

She shook her head. Bad people came in all shapes and sizes. She knew that from personal experience.

She leaned forward and clicked open the second article titled *Wife of Police Administrator Passes.* In the accompanying photo, the green grass of a cemetery's rolling hills glistened in a morning sun. The caption read, *Sunday funeral at Morningview Cemetery—Virat Rahane photography.*

She coped the URL of the photo and sent it to her email.

In her notebook she wrote, *dead wife,* and underlined it. The two words sounded sinister. Especially in relation to an elusive, powerful man. It was too hot in the stacks to shiver, but she felt cold.

She slowly wrote: *Philadelphia. Funeral.* Because she'd found a new angle worth exploring. She'd promised Dom she would stay away from the Filthy Five and promises were meant to be kept.

Chapter Five

Late that afternoon, Dom closed the door quietly, flipped on the fluorescent lights, and took in the garage's familiar smell of motor oil. She'd parked the Lancia in the driveway to give herself more room to work. Against the far wall, she'd set up a well-used folding table and hung a large corkboard on the nail protruding from the wall. It wasn't the first time she'd used the garage as a working space, but it was the first time she'd used it for her own personal investigation.

She peered at the lowest shelf of a shelving unit. The black lids of two large plastic containers stared back.

She placed a finger to her carotid artery and focused on her heartbeat. It felt steady. *Calm for now,* she told herself.

When Stewart died and Esther left, Aunt Lucille had moved fifteen-year-old Domini and ten-year-old Beecher into a sparsely furnished apartment above a Brooklyn bakery. The children had arrived with two cardboard boxes of family documents and three boxes of clothes. Eight years later, when they moved to this house, Dom had transferred the documents into the two plastic containers she now slid from the shelf. She hefted the first box onto the table, sliced the tape, and lifted the lid. She began lifting out stacks of papers and manila folders and set them across the tabletop. *After all these years, it's time to get this done.*

An hour later, all the documents were stacked in three piles. The first pile contained documents related to Stewart, Esther, and their marriage, including legal documents, bank statements, and records on the rental property she had grown up in. Stewart's death certificate had faded to a light yellow and she had stared at it a long time. At sixteen years old, she had received the letter from the life insurance company a year after his death. Even as a teen, she understood the bureaucratic language. There would be no payouts since her father had committed suicide.

She lifted out a manila envelope and slipped open the flap. Inside were two photos. In the first, a young Stewart wore a sharp black tuxedo with a red rose under a wide smile. He was holding a young Esther's hand. Her hair had been pulled up in a smooth knot, her slim white dress still seemed stylish, and her smile appeared natural and happy. In the second photo, a toddler Stewart sat on his mother's lap. Stewart had been an only child and by all accounts his mother had doted on him. That motherly love had forged a confident young man full of optimism.

The same could not be said of Esther. Esther's father, a farmer in Kansas, had been an enigma. Dom had faint memories of his one visit when he had been cold and aloof. Esther's only sibling was Aunt Lucille. The less she had to think about Aunt Lucille, the better.

Dom slipped the photos back into the envelope.

At the bottom of the first pile, Dom found a smaller envelope with two sheets from a psychiatrist in Brooklyn dated two years after Stewart and Esther's marriage. She skimmed the headings. *Neurocognitive disorder. Dissociative disorder. Depersonalization disorder.*

Only once had her father mentioned the doctor assessments: there was nothing they could do. Apparently, they were able to provide fancy words for a mother who sat on a couch, oblivious to her kids, uncaring about her surroundings. Anger crept into her veins, and she slipped the paper to the bottom of the pile.

The second pile was smaller. Much smaller. It held everything their father had collected on herself and Beecher. Their birth certificates with hospital time stamps were neatly pressed between two cardboard pieces. Beecher's preschool graduation certificate was between four elementary school report cards. Notifications reminded of upcoming dental and doctor appointments and two yellow passports verified vaccines. She felt the edges of photos within a small white envelope and left it sealed. She was well aware of what she and Beecher looked like before their life had been turned upside down.

She slid over an empty container, replaced the first two piles of personal documents and stored it back in the shelf where it would likely stay for another fifteen years.

Staring at the remaining pile, she stretched and cracked her neck.

When she was thirteen years old, Stewart Walker had explained that he wanted to become a detective. He had a stack of textbooks he would read at night and he began bringing home folders that he locked in his bedroom closet. Those files, now spread haphazardly across the table, appeared to be unsolved cold cases.

The next few days, weeks, and months would be spent chasing down the secrets hidden in Stewart's collected documents sitting on the table. Elusive clues and twisty rabbit holes would consume frenetic days and long nights. Hopefully, the picture of a crime would emerge in which Stewart Walker was the victim and Velk was the perp. From that, a motive would surface and the jigsaw puzzle would fit together.

She blew out her cheeks. It was when the picture of a crime fell into place, that the Agent in pursuit began to feel the victim's fear.

Two hours later, another three piles were lined up across the table. Tacked on the corkboard were three labels *College student (1995), Drug bust (1997), and Motor stop (1998)*. The corresponding piles represented documents, press clippings, sketches for each case. The first involved the murder of a young college student in her dorm room in 1995, the second centered around a drug bust in the lower East Side in 1997, and the third contained documents related to a 1998 incident between a motorist and two undercover NYPD in Astoria on a drive near the East River.

Dom stepped back and stared at the wall. Were these simply case studies he was using as he prepared to advance to detective rank or were these cases more significant? Had Stewart been digging into cases that eventually led to the fateful night of the Filthy Five in 1999?

Her phone vibrated and she slipped it from her jean pocket.

Lea Peck greeted her. "Boss chick, how's it going?"

"Ok, it's ok. What's up?"

"I'm back in the office."

She meant the NY FBI Field Office downtown in the Javits Building. Lea's desk was in the corner of the 8th floor's huge open plan. Dom could almost hear the air-conditioning units in the background. "Did you get any sleep?"

"Oh yeah, after I left you guys, I came home for a catnap for an hour. I feel great now."

Dom couldn't remember when a nap was enough to make up for a missed night. Youth was wasted on the young. "And?"

"I'm just seeing how you're doing."

She turned from the corkboard. "Starting at the beginning. I've pulled out old stuff. Stuff Beecher and I have been lugging around like turtle shells."

Lea chuckled. "'It is good for a man that he bear the yoke in his youth.' It's from Lamentations."

Dom smiled. "There's a book called Lamentations?"

"Oh yes. The Lamentations of Jeremiah. It's about the destruction of Jerusalem and the Temple. Very dark. All about learning from your mistakes."

"How do you even remember all of it?"

"Oh, they cram that shit in your brain. Trust me."

They paused to let the lighter moment resonate before Lea returned to the topic. "So, our working theory is that your father was set up and that it wasn't a suicide."

"Correct. New theory. Stewart was the victim. The sting was the crime."

"Velk is our first lead."

"Correct."

"A crazy-ass lead. I mean, this is crazy if it's related to Velk."

"Agreed." Her phone vibrated and the screen said *ADIC*. It was her shorthand for Assistant Director in Charge of the FBI's New York Office, Jules Fontaine. She said, "Fontaine's calling."

"Oh dang." Lea hung up.

Dom clicked open on the waiting line. "Walker."

"Agent, where are you?"

"Home."

Fontaine's voice was tight. "I need you over in Jericho. Long Island. There's a missing kid. A local CARD team has been on-site since this morning." He meant an FBI Child Abduction Rapid Deployment (CARD) team had been dispatched. Most likely to the kid's home. The team would have been sent soon after the family called in the missing child.

She turned to the table and the corkboard.

He said, "I've told them one of our best is on the way."

The job came first. The job always came first. *Fidelity. Bravery. Integrity.* "Yes, sir."

"I'll have one of the agents on-site fill you in while you drive." He read out a street address.

She turned and strode toward the kitchen door. "Copy that. I'm en route."

Part II

or did I snare you on my sharper edges
as a bird flying through cobwebbed trees at sun-up
carries off spiders on its wings?

—Lola Ridge, "Secrets"

Chapter Six

KIEV, UKRAINE

Police Officer Ionna Moroz sat on the balcony watching the early morning exercisers in the park, sipping a tea and smoking her only cigarette of the day. A swarm of pigeons took flight and banked by the corner of her building.

She had found the center city apartment two years ago through family friends, and while the building was the bleak Brezhnev style, the fifth-floor balcony was a rare gem. She also forgave the building's lack of elevators because she could walk to the police headquarters and the rent was only a third of her paycheck.

She was crushing the butt in the ashtray when a bang hit her front door. Startled, she set down her tea and rushed to pull on a sweater over her pajamas.

A handsome woman in her mid-forties with natural blond hair and blue eyes stood in the dark hallway. "*Pani* Moroz?"

It was the more familiar title of Miss rather than the rarely used Officer. Ionna nodded.

The woman looked behind her. "Sorry to bother you. May I come in?"

Ionna hesitated.

"Olav Shvets sent me."

Olav was a college friend and one of the few that knew Ionna's first secret: she had skipped two years of secondary school and graduated college early at eighteen. As a result, she had been inducted as the first wave of 2,000 new recruits in 2015 at the very tender age of twenty. She creaked open the door.

The blond stepped inside carrying a big black purse that weighed heavy on her shoulder.

Ionna eyed the woman suspiciously and closed the door. Her second secret was that she had been part of the Euromaidan protests against President Yanukovych and was lucky to have never been caught or identified. Even Olav didn't know that.

The blond set the hefty bag down as she sat on the small couch. "My name is Nadiya Omelchenko. My family is from Kiev. We are from here. We have been here a long time."

"Yes?"

"Something has happened. I need your help. My sister, Aneta, and her husband were murdered last week while they were leaving a restaurant. They stepped out to the street. Their driver was there. They were about to get into the car, but another car raced past. Someone leaned out the window. With a gun. Shot them. Both."

"Oh, I'm terribly sorry."

"Yes, it's been shocking." She shook her head. "They died instantly. They fell there. To the street. It took the police a long time to come. I understand there was a crowd."

"Here in Kiev?"

"Yes, over in Pechersk."

It was a historic and wealthy neighborhood. "I haven't heard of that incident. It is a different precinct. I don't work there. Have they apprehended any suspects?"

"No. And they have not provided us any information—"

Ionna held up her hand. "I'm a patrol officer. I'm not a detective. I won't be able to help you get any more details—"

"That's not why I'm here." With both hands, Nadiya reached into the bag and hefted out a polished wooden box the size of shoebox. Its shiny lock had been opened. "I went to their apartment last night. The detectives had finished there. They let me in. It was so neat inside, despite the police having been there. My sister, she is very tidy. She keeps—kept—her place very clean. Always." Tears dropped down her cheek. "I walked through their apartment. So many things that I remembered. Paintings, books. It smelled like her. I wanted to walk out, come back, and it all be the same as it was before last week. She is my only sibling. Just the two of us. It's always been just the two of us."

Ionna sat in a chair to listen.

Nadiya shook her head to regain composure. "Growing up, our father collected keepsakes from World War II, mostly items from the Ukrainian Insurgent Army that fought against the Nazis and Soviet Union. He kept his treasures in two army trunks in a hallway closet. This collection of his, it annoyed my mother. She never touched those trunks. As kids, Aneta and I would hide things down in them. Things we didn't want our mother to find. Like special rocks, or trinkets. Sometimes we'd hide chocolate down there, but my father, he would find the sweets and eat them." She wiped her tears. "Last night, I don't know how I knew, but I discovered one of my father's trunks was in Aneta's closet. Under her dresses." She pointed to the polished box. "I found that box, in the bottom of the trunk. It was locked. But I knew, I just knew, she would have the key in the apartment. I finally found it in a silk pouch hidden with her bras."

Ionna watched her.

"I need to know what this is all about."

"I, uhm, that's not what I do."

"We believe Aneta's husband, Greigor, was connected to the underworld. Standard *biznesmeni*." She said it with the disgust of a sister likely murdered for Greigor's criminal affiliations. "Greigor was ok. Not nice. Not mean. Treated her fine, but not great. I would have known if he abused her. Husbands. Men." She shrugged as if it was accepted that men would not meet expectations, then nodded to the box. "For her to have hidden this box of mementos and the key, it meant something dear to her."

Ionna held up her hands. "I'm not a detective."

Ignoring her, Nadiya opened the lid to the box and pulled out a yellowed sheet from a newspaper. "This is dated 1996. Aneta didn't marry Greigor until three years later. She was abroad from 1996 through end of 1998. She and Greigor married six months after she returned home to Kiev."

"No, really. I'm not a detective."

Nadiya set the newspaper on the table. "Yes, but you are a junior officer in the Ukrainian police force."

"That's true."

"Then you have access to records and files and officials that I do not."

"That's true."

"And you are underpaid."

Ruefully, Ionna nodded. "Yes, that's also true."

"I want to pay you for moonlighting detective work. I believe it will require your official connections. Also, Olav said you were the smartest person he had ever met. Not man. Not woman. He said you were the smartest *person* he had ever met. That is why I want you to help me. *Pani*, my family is not sentimental. Our sensibilities are very practical. My sister, God rest her soul, put this in a hiding place because it was special. I need to find out what it is about."

Tears flowed freely now. She pulled out her cell phone and opened a selfie of herself with a very pretty blond. "This is Aneta and me last year." She flipped to another image. In it, Aneta was in her twenties, blond hair, blue eyes, and strikingly full lips even more pronounced for the bright red lipstick. She was objectively gorgeous.

Nadiya set down the phone. "She was always beautiful. In her twenties, Aneta was a model and traveled the world. She lived in Paris and Rome. She once went to New York. She would send the most wonderful letters about her life. About the parties, and the boys. She would describe walking down the runway in these silky dresses. She loved to dress up. Sometimes the designers liked her so much they would gift her a dress, or a blouse. She had many in her closet." She blinked at a memory. "When I was in her closet, looking through the army trunks, her dresses, they swept my face. I could smell her perfume."

Ionna waited patiently. She often waited with traumatized victims at crime scenes. She found courage in being able to share the moments of raw pain with a stranger, as if the rare act of intimacy reinforced the bonds of humanity.

"My parents, like most, struggled to provide while we were growing up. Aneta sent money to us. That money kept food on our table and allowed me to go to college. I am a graphic designer now. I have a good career. Her money, her commitment to us, that allowed me to succeed. She took care of me." She leaned back exhausted. "I must do this one last thing for Aneta. I must."

Ionna leaned over the box. "May I?"

"Of course."

Ionna lifted the lid and her mouth fell open. Stacked in rows were polished, thin gold bars, each one inch by two inches. "Oh, my."

Nadiya said, "Yes. I know. It is something."

Ionna lifted one up in the early morning sun. Stamped across the front was an ancient Greek or Roman woman holding a cornucopia that spilled coins. On the reverse side was a stamp of *PAMP 10 oz*.

Nadiya said, "There are forty there. I looked it up last night. An ounce of good gold is about $2,000."

Ionna whistled. The gold inside the box was worth 750,000 US dollars. Give or take.

Nadiya nodded sadly. "It's blood money. I'm sure of it."

Ionna set the bar down.

Nadiya, said, "I will give you one of those bars if you help me."

This time, Ionna mentally whistled. $20,000 for moonlighting was an overwhelming enticement. She may not be a detective, but she was a poor police officer.

Alongside the bars was a small black velvet jewelry box. She lifted it up and pried it open. Inside was an unusual pendant of thin gold wire twisted back on itself many times to form an angel with outstretched wings. It hung from the gold chain.

Nadiya shook her head. "I have never seen it before."

Ionna sat back and took stock of the contents. "A broad sheet of a newspaper, a necklace, and gold bars worth a lot of money. You think this means something other than just a stash for a rainy day?"

"My sister is—was—wealthy. She was not in need of such a stash. No, this is something personal. Our family may not be sentimental, but we appreciate a good symbolism. This is a box of secret memories." She wiped her nose. "Will you help me?"

It was quite a mystery. A very personal mystery for Nadiya. And a $20,000 mystery for Ionna. "Let me do some initial research. If I can help, I will call you."

"Really?"

"Yes. I can't promise anything, but I can at least try."

"That's more than I can ask."

Using her phone, Ionna took photos of the contents before Nadiya returned them to the box and slipped it in her black bag.

Nadiya handed her a bright red business card. "Thank you, *Pani*. Truly. From my heart."

Ionna nodded, not sure at all that she deserved that trust or the thanks.

Chapter Seven

The Special Agent that called Dom as she sped along the Belt Parkway was a frazzled guy named Fred. "Boy's name is Edgar Collins. Six years old. White. Suburban."

It was an interesting fact. The vast majority of child victims of stranger abductions were girls. "Copy that. Tell me what you got." Child abduction was her specialty.

"I'm sending a photo."

Her phone vibrated and she lifted it quickly to peek. In emergencies, some rules were worth breaking.

Edgar Collins had shaggy blond hair over brown eyes and a devious grin. His thin face established he was skinny.

Fred said, "Taken from Collins family home. One-floor rancher. Family believes he was taken between midnight and 8 a.m."

It was 8 p.m. Edgar had been missing for almost 12 hours. Only about one out of ten thousand missing children reported to the local police was not found alive, but of those killed, roughly seventy-five percent were slain in the first three hours.

Fred continued. "Father is Brad Collins, a real estate agent, thirty-six years old. Mother is Frances Collins, thirty-four, nurse. Last night, Friday, the family was hosting a large anniversary party last night for Frances' grandparents. Guests began arriving Thursday. Out-of-towners staying at various hotels. At the house, lots of relatives and friends dropping by, coming and going. Party started at 8 p.m. at a local golf club. Kids under the age of ten stayed at the Collins residence for a sleepover. They had a teen babysitter."

"Copy that." Statistically, Edgar was more likely to have been taken by a relative. Less than a quarter of child abductions were done by strangers. If the child was abducted by a family member, ninety-nine percent of the children were returned alive. If it were non-family, then roughly twenty percent of the children were not found alive.

"The party ended at 1 a.m. Brad tucked in the seven kids on the couch and in sleeping bags in the basement. Then he carried Edgar up to his room. Tucked him in. Mom was up at 8 a.m. this morning to start cooking brunch. At 9 a.m., Dad discovered the empty bed and open window in Edgar's room. Local LE called us by 9:40 a.m." He meant local law enforcement.

The response by local law was good. The sooner the FBI CARD team was on the crime scene the quicker they could protect the integrity of the evidence. People's memories were more accurate and more reliable in the hours following a kidnapping. Get in. Interview the family. Seal their memories. Follow the leads.

But it was unusual that they had called in Dom. CARD teams had a ninety percent success rate of retrieving a child once they'd been called in. It was only when they hit dead ends did they call in HQ specialists.

She asked, "Amber alert?"

"Went out at 0930."

The Amber Alert had gone out within thirty minutes to radio, tv, road signs, cell phones, and other data enabled devices. That was nice timing on their part. Quick.

Fred expected her next question. "No roadblock."

The kidnapper had, at max, an eight-hour jump on them. The car was likely long gone from Jericho. "Understood. Canvassing?"

"Yeah, local LE has been at it."

"How far?"

"So far they've covered a ten-block grid. Nobody's seen anything."

"Middle of the night."

"Exactly."

"Social media?" The FBI local office and local police would have posted BOLOs or "be on the lookout" notices across Facebook, Twitter, Instagram, and TikTok.

"Our team is on it."

She said, "Sounding as good as it can be."

"Still nothing." He sounded defeated. "When you get here, the extended family is all here. Brad. Frances. Four grandparents. Frances' sister and her boyfriend. Single brother. Brad's brother and wife. Four cousins under twelve years old. All have been interviewed."

It would have been a big task. Well done on local CARD team. "Copy that."

"Ask for Tully, Sean Tully, when you get here."

"Thanks, Fred."

"See ya soon."

She pressed the button for speed dial for Lea.

Lea answered with a simple, "I heard. I'm just pulling into Penn Station. I'll head to Javits."

"My value add will be short-lived. They have a full team on site. If I can't help in the next few hours, they won't need me anymore."

"Well then, let's go get Edgar."

Forty-five minutes later, she pulled through the quiet town of Jericho, cornered onto the family's street, and parked at the end of the block. As she approached the house, she counted six dark Bureau sedans lined up by the curb. The black and white house with a connected two-car garage sat back on a deep lawn.

Per protocol, a Jericho uniformed officer stood security at the front door. She flashed her creds and he nodded her past.

The living room was quiet and ripe with pain and shock. A woman with swollen, red eyes sat motionless on a floral green couch, staring vacantly through the front window. Trauma victims present a number of symptoms from disbelief, confusion, anger, guilt, and shame. It was a heady cocktail that the brain struggled to decipher. In quiet moments, victims often disassociated. *This must be Frances, Edgar's mother.*

An older couple, presumably Frances' parents, sat in two armchairs on the other side of the room. The grandmother was rocking herself. The grandfather sat stoically.

No one looked up.

Dom shut the front door and followed a low din down a dim hall.

In the dining room, six members of the CARD team sat around a table loaded with laptops. They were scanning the airwaves and social media. One was on a cell phone rattling off directions to the local canvassing crew. Two agents stood over a credenza, comparing maps on screens. In the middle of the table, in the position of horror honor, was the house landline and the charging cell phones of the mother and father. The tense wait for the ransom call was in full swing. Again, no one noticed her.

In the kitchen, a big guy with a Ceesar ring of hair motioned her in as he hung up a call. Special Agent in Charge Sean Tully held out his hand. "I'm Sean Tully. Thanks for coming."

"Walker. Dom Walker."

His face was grim. "No ransom, no call, no email. Nothing on social."

The fact that they hadn't gotten any leads wasn't good. She nodded. "Never hurts to have some fresh eyes."

"It's worth a shot. Fontaine said your record is good. He actually said excellent."

She shrugged. Her success rate only mattered up until the last case. Today was all about getting Edgar back. "That the mother and her parents in the living room?"

"Yeah, the father's side is in the master bedroom. The kids went to a neighbor's. Something like twelve of them. Big family. We've been in a lull for about two hours now. They're keeping it together but barely. Our psych specialists have interviewed everybody." He looked around to make sure no one could hear. "Our guy didn't get a vibe from any of them..."

She raised her eyebrows.

He eyed her back. "Only strange lead was the mother's younger sister who was out drinking with her boyfriend and friends. They went out last night after the party. She and the boyfriend came back pretty drunk at 2 a.m. Maybe somebody followed them home looking to target a mugging. Or maybe an easy home burglary. I've got two local LE down at the bar asking around. But it feels like a long shot."

It was a long shot. They both knew it. She said, "Copy that. Have either of the parents broken?"

"Mother has been crying and subdued. Father has angered up, I think, three or four times."

"His anger seem normal?"

"Yes. Raw. Instantaneous. He quieted quickly. I don't like him for it."

She nodded.

"We're going on the news and radio this evening. Media will loop through midnight. That's why I called Fontaine."

She had roughly three hours of quiet time before the television crews arrived and things got frenzied. "I'll start with Edgar's parents?"

He nodded.

Chapter Eight

The deli counter of the FBI Javits Building was an homage to the 1980s. The stale wrapped sandwiches in the case were either chicken or tuna salad on white bread. Occasionally there was an egg salad on wheat but those went fast. The selection of bagged snacks were cheap, year-old knockoffs. The sodas in the large coolers were full sugar. There wasn't a diet can in sight.

The only reason agents frequented the cafeteria was because the coffee was exceptional. Thick, dark, and fully loaded.

Lea Peck was waiting in a long line when she noticed Special Agent Owen Whyte approaching. *Lord, you have given the world a very fine specimen of a man.*

He grinned as he got closer. "Lea Peck."

"Special Agent Owen Whyte. You look well and truly recovered. And as always, are a sight for sore eyes."

Last month, Owen and Dom had worked a case that ended in a shootout. Owen had taken a bullet to his shoulder. "And you."

She looked him up and down. "Uhm, hmm. Not in the way I mean it."

He winked at her. "You never know."

She wagged a finger. "Listen, Whyte, do not tease me with those blue eyes. I know your one true intention and it is not my fine self."

He conceded with a shrug. "You see right through me."

"I see enough. You've got a good soul, Agent."

"For whatever good that gets me."

"We'll see." It was her turn to wink.

He fell in line behind her and they shuffled toward the coffee counter.

She asked, "You back on?"

"No, they still have me out on leave."

She gave him a curious look. "So, you're just coming around the office cause you like it?"

He chuckled. "I go crazy sitting at home. I come in to check the latest."

"Uh-huh. That seems weird."

"Sitting in a lonely apartment seems weirder."

"Don't you have any hobbies?"

"Oh, yeah. Just none that I can do with a shot up shoulder."

"And no friends you can visit with?"

"Most people I know have jobs."

He had a point. "And I can take it you don't have a girlfriend?" She gave him a knowing smile.

"You know I don't."

She gave him another wink.

He asked, "How is she?"

His crush on Dom was adorable. "Now, that one. She is always busy. Always, that girl."

"On what?"

"We're on a Long Island kidnapping case at the moment. Boy. Six years old. I'm just coming down for some juice."

He shook his head. There wasn't much to say.

She asked, "How's the bullet hole?"

"It's less of a hole and more of a scar at this point. Still have some physio to do, but it's healing nicely."

"Does it hurt?"

"Medium."

She asked, "Your first?"

He chuckled. "Oh yeah. Forensic accountants aren't normally getting shot. You ever?"

"Not yet. But I'm ready. 'Be of sober spirit, be on the alert.' That's from Peter."

"Lea Peck. You are one of a kind."

Ain't that the truth? "Amen."

Five minutes later, with coffee cups in hand, they headed to the elevator.

Coming toward them down the hallway were Special Agents Frank Fritz and Darren Fan. Good ole Fumble and Drop. She mumbled, "Ugh."

Fumble slowed and a creepy smile crossed the lower half of his face. "Hi, Lea."

Why's he always gotta be so sleazy? "Agent Fritz. How are you?"

"Good, good. How *you* doin'?" He sounded like Joey from Friends. It wasn't a compliment.

"Yeah, good."

"How's Agent Walker?"

Fumble had the hots for Dom. He was always trying to get up in her business. "She's fine. Just fine."

Next to her, Owen stiffened.

Fumble did a once-over on Owen. "She sort that journalist case?"

"Oh, yeah. Done."

"I heard she came in line of fire."

Owen didn't say a word.

Lea nodded. "Yeah. She's fine."

"What she working on now?"

"This, that, and the other. Whatever the Bureau hands out, you know?"

"I hear ya." He chin nodded to them both before starting down the hall with a last throw, "Let her know I was asking."

"Sure, sure, Fritz."

Over his shoulder, Owen watched their retreat. "You guys get that a lot?"

Adorable. "Exactly what, Agent Whyte?"

"That kind of attention?"

"Females make up twenty percent of Special Agents. What do you think?"

"Who is that?"

"We call 'em Fumble and Drop. I worked with them last year on an OC case." She meant organized crime. "Fumble's had a hard-on for Dom ever since she started."

"Oh, yeah?"

"Yeah."

They reached the elevator lobby and sipped hot coffees.

He asked, "They ever work an investigation together?"

She glanced sideways. "Nice code. No, my man, they never hooked up. In fact, last year, I told Fumble he was wasting his time. That I've never known my girl to shit where she works."

Owen said, "Fumble doesn't appear to have taken your advice to heart."

"Yeah, well, who can blame him?"

"He needs to back off."

Cocky. She grinned. "Crushes are so cute. My dear boy, unless you haven't noticed, you ain't got no claims."

"Not yet."

So cocky. "I like your attitude, Whyte."

An empty elevator arrived and they stepped in. The closing door cocooned them in silence.

Owen asked, "Is she ok? Otherwise, I mean?"

She shrugged with exaggerated indifference.

Owen caught it. "What?"

So cocky and so observant. "Nothing."

"What is it?"

"She's fine."

"What then?"

"She's just distracted."

"With what?"

"Nothing."

"With what?"

She sighed. "Something personal."

His mouth dropped open.

She chuckled. "No, not like that. She's single as a red rose in an empty snowy field. And, no, I'm not supposed to be telling you that, but, yes, I am telling you that."

He looked concerned. "Then what?"

"Something with her family."

The door opened on the fourth floor and Lea stepped out.

He followed. "Lea?"

Lea looked around for prying ears and lowered her voice. "Look up the Filthy Five."

He smiled.

"What?" she asked.

"I'm a forensics accountant. I chase shit down all day and all night. Are you under the impression that I haven't done my homework on Special Agent Domini Walker?"

Lea whistled. "Damn, I really like you."

"So, what about the Filthy Five?"

"She wants to open a cold case."

"She thinks what went down was crooked?"

Lea shrugged.

"That implies some kind of setup."

She raised her eyebrows.

"Which means she thinks her father may have been innocent."

She kept her eyebrows raised.

"How can I help?"

"It's not official."

He said, "I got that part. How can I help?"

"She'd be pissed if you got involved. At this stage."

"Yeah, that's not what I asked."

Lea rubbed her lower lip with her knuckles. "You don't give up, do you, Whyte? Slightly dogged."

"It's a problem."

"All right then. I'm gonna give you a name. It's someone we need details on, the likes of which you are rather good at finding."

"Hit me."

She looked around again before whispering, "Dartanian Velk."

A look of confusion swept his face before his eyes widened. "Now LA, formerly NYPD?"

She nodded. "Yup. That one."

"No way."

"Way."
"Oh, shit."
"Oh, shit, indeed."

Chapter Nine

Dom had coaxed Edgar's mother, Frances, to the screened back porch and placed a glass of water and a plate of crackers on the table. Frances ignored the table and stared across the backyard. In situations like this, mothers often didn't eat for days.

Dom settled across the table. "My name is Domini Walker. I am a Special Agent with the FBI. You can call me Dom."

Red eyes stared at the back fence.

"I know you've already been interviewed. I'd just like to follow up on that."

The eyes slid toward a swing set.

Gentle patience was the best approach. "I know you probably don't want to talk anymore. But lots of time we can get additional information from a second interview."

Frances let out a deep sigh. She was hearing Dom, just not responding. That was good. "Frances, I have gotten a lot of kids back."

The red eyes shifted toward her.

"If you help me, I will do my best to get Edgar home."

Red eyes blinked.

"Let's talk about something simple. Why don't you tell me about last night?"

Her voice was scream scratched. "A year. We've been planning for a year."

Dom nodded encouragingly. "It sounded like it was a lot of planning."

"Yes." Frances remained very still. Such stillness could be caused by any number of reasons, but shock was one of them.

"I can imagine. A big anniversary party for your parents."

"We said for a year, a big weekend. What we told everyone."

"That's nice of you and your family to mark the occasion."

Frances turned back to the swing set and her voice was distant. "Mark the occasion."

"Can you tell me some more about the party planning?"

She turned back slowly. "Picked dates. Made reservations."

"You did that mostly?"

"Yes. I did it. Invitations."

"Nice. That's really nice. A very generous gift for your parents."

Frances shrugged. "It was meant to be, yes."

"Lots of guests coming from all over?"

"Lots."

"When did people start to arrive?"

Frances looked up and to the left. "My parents came Tuesday." A left glance could indicate the truth. But it was an unreliable tell.

"How did they get here?"

"They drove."

"What time did they arrive on Tuesday?"

Again, she glanced up to the left. "Seven. At night. We had dinner."

"Good. You're doing great, Frances."

Interviewers looked for a number of indications of deceit. A person's natural way to release anxiety or tension manifested as movement, often a petting move. But Frances was still extremely motionless. She was not presenting anxiety over deceit, likely muffled by the traumatic nature of the situation. A better way to get at deceit would be to delve into details. "What did you have to eat when your parents arrived?"

Finally, Frances looked at her. "Lasagna. I got it from the store."

"During the week, when did the other guests start arriving?"

Frances was watching her now. "Thursday. In and out."

"Family friends came and went?"

"Yes."

"All these folks know your parents?"

Her resistance had been overcome. "Yes. My parents are very social. We moved here from Ohio when we were young. They RV in the summer. Go see their friends around the country."

"That's nice, really nice. And who is staying here?"

"Mom and Dad. Brad's parents. And Veronica and Devon."

Veronica must be the sister. "What about your brother? He is in town too, right?"

Frances nodded. "Craig's at a hotel. He came from Toronto on Monday. Did some work in the city."

"So, lots of folks dropping in and out during the week."

She nodded.

"Then yesterday. You want to tell me about yesterday?"

Frances leaned her head far back, her face toward the ceiling.

It was a blocking movement. She didn't want to think about yesterday. Dom pressed gently. "Can you tell me about yesterday? Can you tell me what you remember before you left for the party?"

Frances spoke to the ceiling. "The babysitter, Tina, arrived at six. I showed her the pantry. The snacks. The sodas."

It was important to get the interviewee comfortable with a cadence. "Where were the kids?"

Frances lowered her chin and blinked at Dom. "Downstairs."

"Could you hear them down there?"

"Oh yes, they were already loud."

"How many kids down there?"

"Seven plus Edgar. Eight total."

"Cousins?"

"Yes, both sides."

Dom kept the cadence moving. "So the babysitter has arrived…"

"She and I order the pizzas."

"What types of pizza?"

"Two cheese only and one veg. The veg was for the babysitter. She's vegan."

It was a good memory point. So far, Frances appeared to be telling the truth.

"Ok. Then?"

"I took her down to the kids."

Dom said, "Frances, I want to get a sense for the setting.

Pretend I wasn't there. When you went down to the basement, can you describe it for me? What did you see?"

Frances stared blankly at Dom, confused.

Dom pressed. "Just imagine I wasn't there and I need to see and feel it. Can you explain what it looks like down there to me?"

"Uh, there's a big screen television for the kids." Frances wasn't displaying any hesitation or resistance.

"What were the kids doing?"

"Playing video games."

"Which one?"

"Wii. A dance contest." The cadence was consistent. Not enough time between answers to be fabricated.

"What's on the screen?"

"A dancing cartoon girl. Pigtails. Pink dress."

"Were any of the kids in the basement dancing?"

"The three girls. Nancy, Megan, Barb." Frances dropped her face into her hands. Her ability to focus was waning.

Dom proceeded gently. "Ok, you're doing great. Now, can you describe how it smelled?"

For the first time, Frances shook her head.

Dom placed both hands on the table. "I'm just trying to get a sense."

"Uh, popcorn."

It was a very defined detail, a difficult one to conjure up in the moment. "Good. What about sounds? What would I hear if I went down there, like you did?"

"The television was blaring."

"What was it blaring?"

"Music from the game."

"Can you describe the music?"

"Country. Kid country. There was a banjo."

"How about the lighting down there?"

"Overhead. Just the overhead lights, spotlights. And the television."

Dom suspected Edgar had been with the other boys. Her next question was not going to be pleasant. But Frances' answer would reveal a great deal.

Dom said, "And what about the other children?"

Frances swallowed. Her eyes widened and blinked in rapid succession. She was reliving the moment she had last seen her son.

Dom leaned against the back of her chair. *Wait for it, wait for it.*

Frances' mouth cracked open as shock cycled to anger. She wailed, "They were on the couch!" With a crack, she slammed both palms on the table and yelled, "Edgar was there! He was right there!" Frances rose and leaned over Dom, screaming, "What are you doing? Why haven't you found Edgar? Where is Edgar? Edgar!"

Dom held up both palms.

Frances leaned her head back and screeched, "Oh, God, where is Edgar?" She fell into the chair, dropped her head to her hands, and sobbed.

From the kitchen window over Dom's right shoulder, a shadow appeared. It was Special Agent in Charge Sean Tully checking on the commotion from the porch.

Dom was following orders: clear the family members one by one.

The shadow disappeared from the window.

The mother was not involved in the kidnapping.

A few minutes later, Dom found the father, Brad, in the garage leaning over his workbench.

"Mr. Collins?"

He looked up. At least he was responsive.

"My name is Dom Walker. I'm a Special Agent. I've got a few questions as follow up. We like to cover some of the same territory while the memories are fresh."

He nodded.

"You ok to do that?"

"Yes."

"Great, thanks."

They sat in two plastic patio chairs under the light of the garage door opener and she had him describe his Saturday. When they reached the time before the party, she slowed down the cadence. "Can you describe what was happening?"

"Frances took the babysitter and the pizzas downstairs."

"What was the noise level?"

His shoulders sagged under the weight of his sorrow. "All the kids, they were screaming. We laughed about it up here, how loud they were. Kids having fun is the greatest noise ever."

She nodded. "Who was up here with you?"

"Frances' parents. Her sister. We were getting ready to leave for the party."

"Ok, can you tell me about when you came home?"

He closed his eyes. It was his sign of blocking against the emotions of a sensitive subject. It was a good indication he was telling the truth. "I sent Frances upstairs. I went down into the basement to tuck in the kids."

"One way to help bring up important memories is for you to explain what you saw as if I needed the details."

He glanced to her with a confused look. "Ok?"

"Just give me whatever details you remember."

"Ok. Well, the television was blaring. They'd fallen asleep to a movie."

"What movie?"

He said, "Shrek."

Good detail. "How were the kids positioned?"

"Four girls on the floor in sleeping bags with pillows. Beck in the middle. The three boys on the sectional. Under quilts."

"What else?"

"The pizza boxes were completely empty, open on the floor."

"What did you do?"

"I found the clicker. Turned off the movie. Made sure everyone was tucked in."

Keep the cadence. "Did any of them wake up?"

"No."

She asked, "Then?"

"I picked up Edgar. I walked upstairs."

"Did Edgar wake up?"

He cringed and blinked against tears. "No. He sleeps hard. I put him in bed. Pulled up the cover. Made sure his bare feet were tucked under."

Good detail. He was relaying memories, not fabrications.

"Now, imagine I wasn't there in his bedroom. Tell me what you saw."

He squinted. "Uh…the nightlight was on. Baby Yoda nightlight."

"Windows?"

"Uh…" He glanced upwards and left for the memory. "Shades open. I am pretty sure there was moonlight."

"Smells?"

"Edgar smelled like pizza. Like he'd rolled around in it." Another good detail. These were not fabrications.

"Noises?"

"Yeah, a hum. He has an air purifier. Young lungs. We try to keep it clean in there. It was humming."

"And then what did you do?"

"I...uh...I kissed his forehead. Went to bed." The tears rolled down his cheeks.

Dom sensed authentic sorrow. "Frances was in bed?"

He shook his head as if the moment had been an annoyance, but now was pure sorrow. "Snoring. With a whistle." The tears were in free flow. "Oh, god. Oh, god."

She left him with his pain. There was nothing she could do to alleviate the burden.

But it was enough to know that Brad wasn't involved in the kidnappings.

Now, she needed to clear the rest of the family.

Chapter Ten

Special Agent Owen Whyte closed the door to his office and rummaged in his gym bag. Like most Bureau staff, Owen had an unregistered "dumb phone" whose top-up card had been purchased in cash. He leaned back in his chair, spun to face the closed door, and dialed a number on the clam phone that he used two or three times a year.

The male voice that answered was breathy. "Yes?"

Friar, a reformed black hat hacker who now day-traded from a loft apartment in SoHo, had sought out Owen five years ago at a Vegas IT security conference. He had offered his help exclusively to Owen as part of a personalized repentance plan.

Owen said, "I've got one for you."

"Hit me."

"Dartanian Velk. V. E. L. K. Born New York-Presbyterian Brooklyn Methodist in 1964. I need an Equifax run."

Owen had worked on the 2018 investigation of the Chinese

People's Liberation Army hack of Equifax. For months, the company had ignored a warning from the US Computer Emergency Readiness Team within the Department of Homeland Security's Cybersecurity and Infrastructure Security Agency—otherwise known as US-CERT. The Chinese had found the vulnerability in a claims portal, and over a period of three months, had accessed fifty databases and stolen creditworthy data—names, birth dates, and Social Security numbers —on nearly a hundred and fifty million Americans. Owen knew how much information was available around the world to hackers as a result of the Chinese theft.

Friar said, "I'll meet you at the sake bar in an hour."

Out in the sun, Owen slipped on Ray-Bans and strolled the three blocks to the City Hall subway station. Below, the platform was sparsely populated, and he leaned against the wall with his arms crossed. A small crowd of tourists with white running shoes and colorful backpacks laughed at dumb jokes.

When the train arrived, he pushed nonchalantly off the wall and merged with the tourists as they shuffled into the second car.

At the next station, he loped from the second car to the first. It was empty. And no one had followed him.

At Astor Place station's 3rd Street exit, he took the stairs two at a time and headed east on East 9th Street. The vintage clothing shop on the corner of East 9th and 2nd Avenue had a hand cut, square wood sign for *Okiniiri*.

Owen jogged down steep stairs and pushed into a dark interior.

Two sushi chefs yelled out, "*Irasshaimase*" and he nodded politely on his way to the back.

Friar, his thick black glasses facing the front door, sat in the last booth. Dreadlocks hung like a superhero cape around the shoulders of a black leather jacket.

Owen shook his hand, slid into the booth, and ordered a Diet Coke from a pretty waitress.

Once the waitress had set the drink on the table and moved away, Friar said, "Man, you better be careful."

That was some truth. "I appreciate the favor."

"You sure you want to go down this alley? From where I sit, someone like this is a hornet's nest."

"Yeah, I know."

Friar pulled a letter-sized envelope from a chest pocket and slid it to the middle of the rough-hewn wood. "If your case goes official, burn this."

"Of course."

Friar nodded to the envelope. "Mostly the real estate. Stinks hink."

Owen sipped his Diet Coke. "Anything else?"

"Nah, he's smart. As he would be."

"Yeah."

"Those guys know how to hide their dirty."

"Nothing else rings wrong for you?"

"Only the real estate. But you'll see. If this guy is bent, you'll find him." Friar gave him a snide look. "Capone and all."

It was reference to the fact that FBI accountants had brought down Capone on tax evasion. "Got it."

Friar slid to the end of the seat and departed with a final, "Good luck."

Owen flagged the waitress and ordered the chef's daily special, the only polite way to order at *Okiniiri*. She nodded when he asked for the sushi on brown rice: he wasn't the only health-conscious New Yorker.

It was time for him to get in fighting shape. Last week,

the doctor said the shoulder wound only needed three more weeks of rest. That timing fit with the minimum four months he needed to train for the Utah Ironman. The 180km bike and the 42.2 km run sections were the perfect motivation. It was the 3.8km swim on a bunk shoulder that would require the most training discipline. Fortunately, Owen wasn't one to shirk a challenge.

He stared at the white envelope. Any investigation of a senior official like Dartanian Velk would be high profile, both within and outside the Bureau. Friar had been correct. This was a hornet's nest.

But that fact didn't make corruption any less a crime. Over the last five years, Owen had been called in by the Public Corruption program three times to help decipher the evidence of fraud in government contracting and procurement. He'd also supported investigations into crooked border and custom officials who had been bought off by drug and weapons trafficking syndicates. He knew firsthand that elected suspects didn't get free passes.

He placed his index finger on the envelope. He wasn't afraid of a hornet's nest. And he wasn't afraid of taking risks. He was alive today because of Dom and now she needed the precise technical assistance for which he had been trained. Of course, he was going to help Dom. One didn't walk away from those kinds of debts.

He tapped the envelope. At a bare minimum he should flag this to his supervisor. But he wasn't going to do that. Dom Walker deserved a head start on this particular case.

His finger paused at a memory. Only a few weeks ago, on an empty floor of the old warehouse, the muzzle of an M24 had sighted on his nose and a shot had rung out. Before he had lost consciousness, he had a glimpse of Dom's face full of gritty determination.

Two fingertips drummed the envelope. Three days after he had awakened from the shooting, in a rare, unguarded moment in his hospital room, Dom had looked at him with warm brown eyes. Time had stilled. It may have been the drugs or the clicking of the monitors by his head, but in that moment, he realized he didn't want to be anywhere else. He had winked at her and, in return, she had given him a radiant smile. His heart had jumped.

He gave one last tap on the envelope. Owen would suffer the lumps if his supervisor found out about the unofficial inquiry into Dartanian Velk.

The waitress set down a sushi plate and a small sauce bowl.

Ten minutes later, Owen opened Friar's envelope and slid out two printed sheets. A colorful pie chart in various shades of blue compared Velk's credit score—810—to the larger population: Velk was in the slice of the highest two percent of Americans.

A table under the chart listed his annual salary for the last five years.

$250,200 Los Angeles Police Department
$245,000 Los Angeles Police Department
$222,450 Los Angeles Police Department
$216,200 Los Angeles Police Department
$195,003 Philadelphia Police Department

It was good money. Most police officers made $70,000 base pay, but could take home upwards of $90,000 with overtime and added comp. As a senior LADP leader of a force of roughly ten thousand officers and three thousand civilians, Velk's salary was high but not unreasonable.

Below the salary table, a line chart depicted Velk's monthly debt. He carried between $1,000 and $1,300 month-on-month. Slightly above average, but also not unreasonable for a guy making mid-200s.

Owen flipped to the second page. Things got interesting quickly.

Velk's home in a residential area called Brentwood had an estimated value of $4.1 million. Owen whistled.

The Equifax report did not list Velk's monthly mortgage. But it didn't need to. Depending on the size of the initial down payment, Velk's monthly mortgage was very likely in the range of $16,000 and $20,000. Despite the fact that most Americans ignored the general rule that housing costs shouldn't run more than thirty-two percent of your gross monthly income, Velk should be paying a monthly mortgage to the tune of $6,500. Velk was paying a ton more than his salary suggested he could. He was either supremely over-leveraged or he'd put down a whopping deposit.

Owen took a sip of Diet Coke. Either scenario raised further questions.

Friar had been correct about a second point. Velk's real estate assets had a very bad smell.

Chapter Eleven

It wasn't until the fifth interview of a Collins family member that Dom's instincts kicked to high gear. In a blue armchair in the second-floor guest room, Craig Hosier, Frances' brother, sat stiffly. He was a forty-something professor living in Toronto with an unfortunate round face and thin hair. His green eyes were strikingly large and gave him an air of intelligence.

Dom sat on the end of the bed five feet away. "Craig, how are you doing?"

His face was somber and his hands were still on the armrests. "I mean, not great. I mean, this is atrocious. A horrendous nightmare."

"Yes. It's a terrible situation."

"How can I help?"

"I'm interviewing the family again, to see if we missed any clue or piece of evidence. It's better to get these second rounds in early. Memories fade over time."

His body was particularly still. Similar to his sister, there were no movements, no petting, nothing to reassure himself. "Sure. Of course."

"You live in Toronto?"

"Yes. Have been up there ten years."

"What do you do there?"

He clasped his hands in his lap. "I'm a professor. I teach at the university."

She noted that he answered swiftly and with confidence. "What do you teach?"

"Architecture."

"Family? Wife, husband, partner?"

"I'm straight. No girlfriend at the moment. I date, but no one serious."

He was quick to follow her cadence. It indicated a sharp intellect. "Do you visit with family much?"

"I come down to visit about four times a year. Toronto to here is a pretty quick trip. I have friends in the city. I see them when I come down, too."

"When did you get in town this time?"

"I got in Monday."

"And?"

"I checked into the Marriott, took the evening off."

"Do you usually stay here?"

"Normally I do half and half. I'll do a few days here with Fran then some in the city. This weekend, with my parents here, I'm at the hotel in town."

Time to kick the tension up. "I'd like to ask you a few questions about Edgar. When was the last time you remember seeing him?"

There was a slight hesitation and it disrupted their rhythm. "I've been thinking about that. I mean, I don't really remember seeing him yesterday. The day was very busy, lots of errands to do to get ready for the party. I was only here for a second. So, really, I remember seeing Edgar Friday."

"Can you tell me about that?"

His interlocked fingers flayed for a brief moment. "I was in the living room with Mom and Edgar ran through with a Frisbee."

Had his movement indicated anxiety? She slowed. *Let him stew a bit.* "Did you say anything to him?"

"No."

She waited a beat longer than normal. "Huh. Ok."

She ran him through more short questions that elicited details about the party. The music, the food, the guests. He was self-assured in his answers and the tempo continued to be tight. She asked, "Did you drink?"

"I'm not a big drinker."

"Did others?"

"Oh, sure. Frances got lit. Brad was ok. Mom was pretty sauced."

This matched what she'd heard from the grandparents. It was a boozy night for some, not all. "You didn't have *any* drinks?"

"I had a wine with dinner."

"What type?"

He paused, cocked his head. "I told the waiter white. He brought me, I guess, whatever Frances had arranged."

"But it was white?"

His eyes narrowed and he scratched his thigh. His response was slower to come. "Yes."

He was wondering if she was testing him. It was causing him anxiety. "When did you leave the party?"

He was watching her with interest. "When they shut it down. Midnight, I guess."

"What did you do after?"

He frowned and clearing his throat. "I'm sorry?"

There. There was the telltale push back. Craig Hosier had recognized he was being questioned by an FBI Special Agent as a potential suspect. She repeated the question. "What did you do after leaving the party?"

He leaned back and crossed his arms over his chest. "I went down to the hotel bar."

Time to dance. "Is it a good bar?"

His face showed wariness. "It's ok."

"Can you describe it for me, as if I wasn't there?"

"I'm sorry?"

"Can you describe it for me, as if I wasn't there?"

"Uh, it was busy. I'm not sure I remember much of it."

When confronted with this approach to recall questions, an innocent person would often express confusion, but not resistance. A guilty person began to look for an exit from the interview. "A lot of people there?"

"Yeah."

"How many?"

His head shifted away from her. "I'm sorry?"

He was physically and verbally blocking her. "How many people were there, give or take?"

He squinted. "Uh, let me see. Maybe twenty, thirty?"

"That's a good number for a hotel bar."

"Yeah. It was busy."

"Did you drink?"

"A soda water."

"Plain?"

He glanced up and to the right. An indication of deception, but not a reliable one. "Two limes."

"What else can you tell me about the bar?"

"What do you mean?"

People who make up stories often can't provide convincing detail. If pressed, it's an uncomfortable feeling. "What material is it made out of?"

"What?"

His resistance was growing. "I'd like you to tell me what you remember from the bar, visually."

"I don't remember what the bar was made of."

"What *do* you remember?"

"I remember people."

She waited.

His brow furrowed and he pulled on his right earlobe. "A couple on my left. A single woman at the end of the bar."

Craig Hosier was showing signs of high anxiety. "What was she wearing?"

"I don't remember."

"What about sound?"

He closed his palm over his cuff to prevent small movements. He knew she was observing him. "I don't remember."

"What about the smell?"

"Uh. Nothing of note."

A shout came from the front door. The news crew was here.

Craig's eyes widened and he exhaled.

The distraction from downstairs was a relief for him. She rose. "Thanks for your help. Let's go be with the family."

He watched her with interest. "That's it?"

"Yeah, that's fine."

His jaw relaxed. He was regrouping. "Are you sure that helped?"

"Yes. Best get down to the front now."

He rose slowly.
She motioned for him to proceed.
He glanced back at her as he walked down the stairs.
She had her suspect.
But she didn't have Edgar.

Chapter Twelve

Two news trucks sat in the street with raised towers. A crew of nine journalists stood in a semicircle around the front steps of the house, their cameramen behind them. Dom stood at the end of the drive by a local police cruiser.

Standing next to a big poster board with a color photo of Edgar with a huge toothy grin and fine strands of wafting hair, Sean Tully spoke first. Tully repeated the specifics twice: the boy was taken from the house in the middle of the night, they believe through the upstairs bedroom window. There had been no luck with canvassing. They were looking for any leads. Telephone lines and social media channels were open. Nothing was too small. He repeated the numbers and social media details.

The radio in the cruiser squawked and the driver turned the volume lower.

Dom stared at the boy's eyes. *I'm here, Edgar. I'm close, aren't I?*

When Brad Collins stepped to the front, the reporters

hollered questions. "Has there been a ransom request?" "Did they have any suspects?"

Next to the father, Sean Tully raised his hand to quiet the crowd.

Brad Collins cleared his throat. "It is Edgar's birthday next month. He turns seven. We have a birthday party planned for him with his friends. The theme is Spiderman. We are renting a trampoline and ice cream maker. Please, we beg you. Call us, turn him over, we won't prosecute if we get Edgar back safely."

Edgar, I'm so close.

Frances stood numbly by her husband with a vacant disassociated stare.

The family standing behind the distraught parents were grim and worn down. Both sets of grandparents were on the verge of tears. Frances' sister still looked green with a guilty hangover. Craig stood stoically staring above the heads of the reporters.

Sean Tully returned to the poster, repeated the numbers, and made a final plea for information.

Edgar, I'm so close.

Craig's eyes dropped to the faces in the small crowd and scanned them, moving slowly from the far left. For second, his gaze met Dom's, but purposefully moved on. It was a manufactured indifference. She had just been interrogating him: he should be afraid of her. But sociopaths blended well, unless you knew what to look for.

I see you. I know you.

The official term was antisocial personality disorder. It was often associated with sociopaths, people who have some conscience, or psychopaths who typically have no conscience. Such individuals had an unusually high ability to deceive. They don't care about right or wrong and they like to manipulate the people with wit or charm. They fail in intimate relationships so tend to be single. Past victims have described them as lone wolves. For Dom, the tell of a disordered person was the ever-present arrogance. They thought they were smarter than everyone else.

You think you've gotten away with it.

Her brain hummed. Everything about Craig Hosier felt manufactured.

Sean Tully turned to the family and ushered them to the front door. Brad took his wife's hand and led her into the house. One of the grandmothers began to cry. The sister covered her mouth as she turned from the reports. Craig stood for a beat, watching the reporters as they gathered in the street by the trucks. He showed no emotion. He did not turn his gaze toward Dom.

Dom tuned out the noise from the street. She relaxed her shoulders and breathed deeply.

Craig was the last to turn into the house and he closed the front door.

Letting her instincts free, Dom began random word association. *Craig Hosier. Alone. Single. Professor. Veneer. Smug. Arrogant. Manufactured.* Her brain skipped. It had skipped on the word *manufactured.*

She took another deep breath. *Manufactured. Constructed. Assembled. Prepared. Premediated. Planned.*

She blinked. *Planned. Craig had planned to abduct Edgar this weekend.*

Her heart thumped. That was the next key. If Craig Hosier had planned to abduct Edgar, how would he have done it?

She turned slowly in a 360, letting her eyes and mind wander. The police cruiser. The cars parked in a line in the street. The news trucks. The green lawn. The black and white house. The connecting garage. The driveway.

Craig would have come in the night from the hotel and walked up the driveway. He would have stepped through the front door. If anyone noticed, it would have seemed normal. Stopping by after the party. *Premeditated.* He would have gone up the stairs to Edgar's room. He would have opened the window to make it look like a stranger. *Arrogant.* He would have scooped up the heavily sleeping boy. He would have walked back down the stairs and out the front door. *Assembled.* How had he transported the boy?

Dom slowed the turn. How had he transported the boy? How could she know that? Did he rent a van? They'd seen the use of vans before. Many times.

She stilled. *A van.*

She strode to the end of the drive and moved down the street away from the noisy trucks as she slid her phone from her jacket pocket.

Lea picked up the call on the first ring. "Hi."

"I've got an idea. But it's a long shot."

"Oh, Saint Christopher, hear our prayers."

"I need you to check the flight records of Edgar's uncle, Craig Hosier. He says he came down on a flight on Monday from Toronto."

"Sure. What are you thinking?"

Dom closed her eyes. "Maybe the flight was a deception, a red herring. If he drove, he would have used a van."

"Did he say what time of day he arrived?"

"Not exactly, but I got the sense it was afternoon. Check the whole day."

Lea went quiet and the keyboard clacked.

Five minutes later, she said, "I'm looking at four airlines that fly direct from Toronto into NY airports. I'm checking them." There was more clacking across the line. "I've got ten flights: six into LaGuardia, four into JFK. I'm ignoring Newark. I'm downloading passenger manifests."

Across the street, from under a shrub, two small feline eyes glinted. Dom wondered how Tinks was doing, but also knew that she didn't need to worry because Beecher was an excellent dog dad. It was her nature to worry.

Lea's voice was tight. "He's here. Delta Flight 4758 arriving 4:45 p.m. LaGuardia."

Shit.

Dom stared at the shrub. The cat had disappeared. A television truck swept past her. "Ok. Let's carry that thought through and do the due diligence. Can you call the Marriott and confirm he checked in on Monday as he claimed?"

"Roger. Stand by."

She was put on a silent hold. The FBI didn't use dentist office music on their phone lines.

The setting sun cast a pink glow across the house and the windowpanes glinted. Inside the dining room, the CARD team would be manning their computers, waiting for tips. Frances was probably on the flowered couch with the grandparents holding vigil. Brad would be pacing in the garage. It was a house heaving with pain.

She hung her head. It never got easier.

Lea came back on with a tight voice. "I spoke to the front desk. Craig Hosier checked in on Monday as he claimed. They have a record of it. Took his credit card information at 6 p.m. His stay is scheduled through the end of this week."

Dom raised her head.

In a second-floor window, there was movement. A curtain had rustled. It had been a curtain falling back into place. As if someone had been watching her then let the curtain drop.

Intelligent. Calculating. Resourceful.

Lea broke through her musings. "What are you thinking?"

Dom stared at the window. That would be the guest bedroom where she'd interviewed Craig.

Lea waited.

Craig had been watching her. Craig had stood in an empty room to look through the window at a suspicious FBI Special Agent hunting a kidnapper.

Untouchable. Impervious. Solitary. Alone. Empty room.

Her brain skipped again. She took a deep breath and rewound the words. *Alone. Empty room.* She said, "Lea?"

"Yes. I'm here, Dom."

"Get the hotel back on the line. Have them check their systems. Did someone check in later on Monday, after shift change? Did a single male check in that night? Maybe late that night?"

"Holy Mother of Fuckers. You think Craig got a second room?" The line went silent as Lea placed her on hold.

The sun had set and shadows crept across the front lawn.

Edgar, I'm near.

The line opened and Lea rushed, "A John Malone checked in at midnight on Monday. With the night staff."

Dom stopped breathing.

"Hotel security is going up to John Malone's room now."

Edgar, I'm coming.

Dom moved slowly along the curb to the end of the drive and closed in on the police cruiser. The officer at the steering wheel noticed her and slid down the window. She turned her back to the house, the phone still to her ear, and used a very calm voice. "Stay normal. Just talk to me normally. We're being watched."

Neither of the men stiffened. True professionalism.

"Driver. I need you to stay in the car but draw your weapon."

She could see his hand slide a gun from its holster.

"Passenger, I need you to casually get out, stretch your arms, and pretend to take a slow, meandering walk around the house. Meandering. As if it's a normal patrol. We're being watched. Understood?"

The police officer in the passenger side said, "Yup."

"When you get to the back, draw your weapon. I need you to cover the back entrance. We may have a runner. Understood?"

"Yup." The passenger side door opened, and the officer stood from the car. He stretched his hands over his head and leaned forward as if cracking his back. Nice and casual. Then he took off at a slow walk around the side of the house.

To the driver, she said, "I'm going to go stand at the end of the drive. In two minutes, can you step out and lean back against the car, as if nothing is happening? Just nice and relaxed against the car, taking a breather."

He said, "Copy."

"Be ready in case the door opens and our perp bolts."

"I got you covered."

With the phone to her ear, she strode slowly toward the street. Darkness had shrouded the shrubs. *Edgar, I'm coming.*

Lea's voice boomed over the phone. "We got Edgar. The kid's alive. Hotel security has hands on him. We got him."

Dom turned toward the house and closed the line.

The police officer stood from the car and leaned back against it casually.

Dom dialed Sean Tully.

He answered. "Tully."

"We've got the kid. He's at a hotel. He's safe. Craig Hosier, the uncle, is your perp. Hosier is upstairs in the guest room."

Sean Tully hung up.

It was over.

Part III

Secrets,
running over my soul without sound,

—Lola Ridge, "Secrets"

Chapter Thirteen

KIEV, UKRAINE

Police Officer Ionna Moroz hustled to work. She only had an hour before she had to hit patrol and she needed to work on the computer. Junior police officers didn't have laptops at home. She rushed through the front entrance of the pink building that housed the General Directorate of the National Police on 15 Volodymyrska Street and jogged up the narrow stairwell to the third floor. Ukraine's police department was in the midst of a youth hiring campaign and headquarters was loud with the influx of new recruits.

Ignoring the loud groups of chatty officers, she dropped her cap on her desk and pushed on the old computer. Its fan whirred loudly.

Earlier, she'd sent the photos of the mystery box contents to her work email and now she stared at the front and back page ripped from the English language *Kyiv Post* dated December 28, 1996. In 1996, the country was still reeling from the monumental fall of the Soviet Union five years earlier. The tumultuous term of the second President, Leonid Kuchma, was marked by scandals and corruption.

Despite the new government's efforts to restrict media, the *Kyiv Post*, through its Pakistani owner, Mohammad Zahoor Sunden, had emerged as committed to editorial independence and frank reporting.

Ionna skimmed the articles.

The New Constitution Guarantees Democracy, Limits Politicians Corruption
The final draft of the new Constitution guarantees democratic freedoms and rights while establishing a Western-style judicial system. Every citizen is guaranteed the right to private property and the right to own land. "We have joined the league of European nations—nations that have chosen democracy and freedom, and there is no going back," said Serhiy Holovatyi, a principal author of the Constitution.

Post Independence Struggles Continue: Economic Hardships on Workers
Many Ukrainians in a variety of sectors, including teachers, doctors and miners, worked without being paid for months. The World Bank found almost 30% of the country lives in poverty. Many hope the introduction of new currency may help the economic woes of Ukraine.

Do we have enough clout to negotiate oil fees with Russia?
Our government wants to get closer to Europe and the West. But Russia and its Commonwealth of Independent States holds us hostage through the oil talks. Moscow has taken a hard line against Ukraine's announcement of increasing prices on transit fees to move oil supplies from Russia to the Czech Republic and Slovakia through the Druzhba pipeline

The State is failing to control organized crime
The absence of strong law enforcement norms or judicial institutions is allowing organized crime to expand. Less than 10% of Ukrainians

polled believe the country is on a path to legitimate rule of law. The port city of Odessa continues to be a source for transnational crime with links around the world from Iran, Afghanistan, Chechnya, and Brighton Beach in New York.

Irina Borisova wins Miss Ukraine Universe
Miss Borisova will represent Ukraine at the Miss Universe championship for a chance to win the title of Miss Universe at Miss Universe 1997, the 46th pageant to be held in May next year. The event will take place at the Miami Beach Convention Center in Miami Beach, Florida, United States.

She got to the end of twenty-six articles and returned to the top to read each one more thoroughly. The single sheet of newspaper presented Ukraine at the beginning of its political turmoil. In the vacuum left behind by the fall of the Soviet Union, ruthless men and powerful criminals—often the same thing—went after the big industries like mining and energy to became billionaire oligarchs, governors, and presidents, like Viktor Yanukovych, the treasonous fourth President who ruled Ukraine from 2010 until the 2014 Revolution. The fledgling justice system couldn't keep up with the criminal elements and everyday citizens were at the mercy of organized crime.

Ionna stared at the image. Why would a glamorous model living overseas save this particular page of this particular newspaper? Had she purchased it from a kiosk in Paris or Rome to feel closer to home? Had something in the news been noteworthy to her? Had she known Miss Ukraine?

Ionna rubbed her eyes. She did not have enough information about Aneta Omelchenko to know which one, if any, of these articles had struck a nerve.

She looked around the busy floor. Secretaries were

typing furiously, patrol officers were organizing their equipment, and detectives were staring at screens or yelling down phone lines. Meanwhile, Police Officer Ionna Moroz had been pretending to be a detective and had spent too much time reading a newspaper as if it would magically deliver clues. It had been a rookie move. If she had been a real detective, she would have known that this particular piece of evidence was too broad to deliver insights. If she had been a real detective, she would have started with one of the other clues in the mystery box.

She shut her computer and jammed her cap on her head. She had a patrol route to get to.

Chapter Fourteen

In the garage, Dom sipped a coffee and focused on the corkboard notes above the foldout table. *College student (1995), Drug bust (1997), and Motor stop (1998)*.

Earlier, she had visited ADIC Jules Fontaine and briefed him on the Edgar Collins case. "He's back with the family. The perp was apprehended in the house."

He had clenched his fists. "The kid's uncle?"

She nodded.

He shook his head. There were no words to adequately describe the amount of terrible people and actions in the world. In the Bureau, you move on. Quickly.

She said, "I'd like to take some time off."

"How much?"

"Three days. Just to get something started."

"Sure." He gave her a questioning look. "Any particular reason?"

She glanced away.

"You doing something I need to know about, Special Agent?"

"I just want to look into something."

"Uh-oh. That's not a good thing coming from you. That's often how you get wrapped up in something."

Dom nodded again.

"I thought we agreed that after St. Chris you'd take it easy."

In the last year, she had been involved in a massive child trafficking ring, the kidnapping of the daughter of a rich New York family, and the murder of a journalist. All the investigations had been hairy. She should take a break. She should. But she couldn't. Not now. "Yes, sir."

"You're lucky you report to me."

It was an unusually direct reporting line, but Fontaine liked having one of his best kidnapping specialists available on his team. "Yes, sir."

"Does this have something to do with your father's history?"

Her heart jumped. "It might."

Fontaine watched her with sad eyes. "You need to close this, don't you? After all these years, you need to close this. For him?"

Be strong. That's what Stewart had told her. She nodded, her throat thick.

Fontaine leaned back in his chair. "This is how I see it: given the subject matter, you're not going to be a hundred percent for Bureau business unless you sew up this wound. But we have the same deal we always have. You come to me as soon as you have something solid."

"Agreed."

He had said, "Ok. Good hunting. See you in three days."

Dom set her coffee on the foldout table and lifted the

first document from the first pile. It was a newspaper article about a nineteen-year-old female college student, Susan Mills, at a small liberal arts college in Staten Island. Susan had been strangled and killed in her dorm room in 1995. The perpetrator had never been found. Susan's body was found by her friend in the morning. The case file contained additional details: there was no evidence of foul play and no suspects; the two detectives noted an open window as the probable source of entry; and Susan Mills hadn't had a boyfriend and no recent altercations of any kind with anyone. A copy of a letter from Susan's father laid out his daughter's whereabouts for the prior twenty-four hours.

Stewart had scribbled a note with the date 1998 across the copy of the father's letter, *"Why didn't we follow this? Did this go anywhere? Did someone check the grounds under any other windows?"*

Dom lifted up a photograph of the dorm room window over shrubs and sidewalk. Stewart must have gone to the crime scene, because the photo was dated 1998.

Dom moved to the next pile of documents related to a 1997 drug bust in the lower East Side. Three teens, Anton Fontaine, Jamaal Mullen, and John Markham were caught selling marijuana near a local high school. Stewart had clipped three newspaper articles and made copies of the files on the three teenagers. He had also pulled court documents and written in red along the margins. *"Where did the three come from? Any common affiliation?"* and *"Nobody tried to find common link."* Stewart had also underlined a comment from the police intake form. *"None of these men have said a word in their defense. - 1998."* She wondered what happened to the three teens.

The final case was a 1998 incident in Astoria on a drive

near the East River that took place between a motorist and two undercover NYPD. The driver, Joseph Rampbell, had noticed the trunk of a Toyota Corolla was open. Rampbell pulled alongside the Corolla, honked, and motioned to the driver. The driver, an off-duty NYPD Officer Zhao, pulled his firearm and shot at Rampbell. Rampbell sustained a wound to his hand as he sped away.

Stewart Walker had collected six articles from the local paper that the shooting had been determined as justified. Stewart had noted, "*On what grounds? - 1998*"

She looked across the three piles. Clearly, in 1998, Stewart had been looking into cold cases. His notes indicated he disagreed with either the investigations or the outcomes. Was there a common theme between the three cases? Were the NYPD officers involved somehow connected? Had he discovered IA was out of line in each? Most importantly, were these somehow related to the Filthy Five?

There was one person who may know.

She lifted her phone and scrolled through the directory. *NYPD Officer Roger Byles.* She pushed the call button.

The voice was that of an older man. "Byles."

"Roger. It's Domini Walker."

"Hi, Dom. How are you?"

"Yeah, ok. Ok. Listen, I, uh, I've been doing some digging."

Silence.

"Stewart brought some of his work home with him. From 1998. There are three files, three investigations. It looked like he was questioning certain aspects. I'm not sure. But it feels very coincidental. Especially the timing."

"Is that right?"

"He was going out to crime scenes. Digging up official

files. I get a sense, maybe...maybe just a daughter's interest to clear her father's name...but I get a sense this may be involved somehow in the Filthy Five case."

"Can you come see me?"

She stiffened. "You home now?"

"Yes."

"I'm on my way."

Retired NYPD Officer Roger Byles had lived in his brick townhome in Park Slope, Brooklyn, for fifty years. His father had lent him the money. Over the years, he'd watched as the neighborhood became increasingly wealthy with fancy cars, toned mothers with sleek hair and expensive strollers, and ritzy restaurants. He'd watched the entire transformation from the comfort of his front porch.

Dom found him where she always found him, in one of two chairs overlooking the park.

She climbed the stairs. "How you doing, Roger?"

"You know, same ails, different day. Can I get you a beer?"

"Better a soda if you got it."

He hefted himself from the chair. "Sure, sure. Take a seat." When he returned with a Sprite, he gave her a tender smile. "It's good to see you. How's Beech?"

"Good. Hard at work at City College. They keep him busy."

"Smart kid."

"Always."

"He got a girl?"

She laughed. "Beecher's always dating somebody. But he hasn't brought any of them home to meet me."

Roger gave her a grin. "He's afraid you won't like them."

She raised the Sprite in salute. "I won't."

"Ha!"

"Seriously, that kid is a genius, he's also funny, he's also an absolute teddy bear. After that Slender-billed vulture got to him, I'm gonna be a little bit more stringent in my oversight of his romantic life."

Roger gave her a quizzical look.

"It's a kind of vulture. It's her nickname."

"The divorce all sorted?"

She let out a big sigh. "Finally."

"And that little girl you got living with you? How she doing?"

"Mila is good." She grinned. "Funny individual but very endearing in her own right."

"How long she gonna stay with you?"

"Don't care. She's good to have around. I'd be fine if she stayed with us until she finishes college."

He gazed out over the park. "The Walkers are good people."

She swallowed. "I'm looking into what happened to Stewart."

"So you said."

"There's been some new information."

"Evidence?"

"No. Not that solid. More a lead. Esther got a letter. One of the Filthy Five confessed to his wife while he was drunk." Her throat constricted. "Said Stewart was innocent."

Roger nodded.

Dom said, "It was weird that Stewart got caught up with them that night. It doesn't really make sense. He was an undercover guy. Solo. Weird they sent him to respond to Gessen's call in. Did you know the other cops in the Filthy Five?"

Roger sipped his beer. "I've run across Gessen a couple times. He isn't right in the head. And I've had some overlap with Belafonte. He's not much. Timid guy. Surprised he's a cop. Gessen's your leader. I looked into that."

She set down the soda on the side table. "What? When?"

"After..." He meant after Stewart had died. "I wanted to know the answers, too. Your father always insisted he was innocent. But when I pressed him on the details, he'd clam up."

"You went to see him?"

"Oh yeah, before the trial and then after."

"He wouldn't tell you the details?"

"Nah. It was like he was...I dunno...protecting something. At one point, I thought maybe he was protecting me, as weird as that sounds."

"And?"

He shook his head. "I hit dead ends. I sniffed around on Gessen and the others. In the files, whatnot. But I couldn't find anything direct." He turned to her. "What have you found?"

"He was looking into three cold cases. A murdered college girl, a teen drug bust, and a driving incident where an off-duty officer took a shot at a civilian."

Roger let those sink in.

"Stewart's notes seem to indicate he was curious about the police shooting being justified."

"Huh."

She raised her eyebrows, "I know, right? And when we met with Esther—"

"You met with her?"

She paused. "Yeah, she came here."

Roger remained silent.

"She said she remembers Dartanian Velk coming round our house, the last year of Stewart's life."

His eyes popped. "Whoa."

"Weird right? Head of IA coming to the apartment of a foot soldier. One who happens to be questioning a ruling on a cop-civilian shooting."

His voice turned soft. "I'm glad you came. That all is adding up."

"To what?"

"He did say something to me. One of those visits. It never made sense, until now. But it sounds like maybe we're talking about something a bit bigger. He said, 'Cops work in groups. Pairs. Two pairs. Always in these connected groups.' I pressed him, but he didn't pursue it."

A chill brushed her arms. "God, it's like he's speaking to me right now."

Roger turned to gaze over the park.

She asked, "Cops work in groups. What does that even mean? Of course most of them are assigned."

"I don't know. It's just what he said. I'll never forget it."

She took a sip to slow her mind. "So, at the time, we've got Stewart looking into cold cases. After the arrests, Stewart claims innocence but doesn't defend himself. One of the Filthy Five now confirms he was innocent. And now there's some tangential connection to Velk."

"Uh-huh. Sounds about right."

She glanced to him. "Sounds a lot like the beginnings of a conspiracy."

"You best be careful, young lady."

They sat for a long time in the warm sun on the porch.

She rose. "I'll keep you posted."
"You better, young lady."
"I will."
"You make him proud every day."
Her eyes stung.

Chapter Fifteen

Owen Whyte sank into the cushions of the armchair in the gently lit basement office of a Chelsea town home. Unlike the office chairs he used during the workday, this was overstuffed and comfortable. It wasn't Freud's carpet-covered couch, but it was damn close.

Eileen Bremmer, her long straight gray hair in a smooth ponytail, gave him a gentle smile. "How are you feeling?"

After the shooting, the Employee Assistance Counselor (EAC) had assigned him a psychiatrist to coordinate a fitness-for-duty examination with the Medical Operations and Readiness Unit (MORU). Until then, he was officially on internal leave, no active assignments.

He raised his wounded shoulder to feel the twinge. "Good. Gets better every day."

"How's the pain?"

"Nothing I can't handle."

"From a one to a ten?"

"The truth?"

She smiled softly. "We aim for truth in here."

"It's about a seven. Mostly."

During his first visit, Eileen had explained that she had thirty years of practicing psychiatry and that for the last ten, she'd worked exclusively with law enforcement. Her specialty was post-traumatic stress. Nothing, she assured him, was outside the scope of their discussions. Agents often struggled with anger management, conflict resolution, coping skills, interpersonal communication skills, and relationships. Everything was confidential. Eventually, when he was fit for assignment, she would work with him to prepare a Bureau psychological evaluation.

Having finished her introduction, she had leaned back in the chair and rested her arms on the armrests.

He had given her a big smile.

She furrowed her brows. "What's that for?"

"My mom's a shrink."

"Ah, I see."

"I'm fine being here. Therapy doesn't scare me."

"That's good."

"It just means you can't shrink me. I've had a lifetime of that."

"I don't shrink anyone. I'm here to have a dialog with you and to help with any unresolved issues that may prevent you from performing your best at work."

"Yeah, I know."

"Our focus is on your well-being. Wherever that takes us."

He had spread his hands in offering. "Let's do it."

They'd covered a lot of territory in five sessions. They'd established that he had some intrusive memories from the event, but the flashbacks were minimizing over time. His physiological reactions when they revisited the event were the normal and expected heart rate spikes. He hadn't been feeling alienated or detached from his friends and family and he didn't have unusual irritability, recklessness, or hyper-vigilance. She deemed his response to the shooting to be healthy.

Today, she asked, "You still refusing pain meds?"

"Yes. You don't have to worry about addiction with me." Like many high-performance athletes, Owen preferred to interpret his aches and pains.

Eileen changed the subject. "Let's discuss a new area of interest. We now know that agent-involved trauma can lead to persistent or distorted issues of blame. I'd like to talk about anyone you may have sensed a feeling of blame. So, for example, perhaps we have a chat about Agent Walker?"

He hid a grin. "I haven't seen her."

"Have you tried?"

He smiled. "Oh, yeah."

She perked up. "How's that?"

"I went down there yesterday. She wasn't around."

"And?"

"I spoke to her team member."

She raised an eyebrow.

"I'm gonna help Dom out."

"Tell me more about that."

He felt warm. "She's looking into a cold case. I'm going to assist."

"Assist unofficially."

"Yes, Doc. Unofficially."

"You seem uplifted by this."

His grin widened. "Oh, yeah."

She smiled at his enthusiasm. "How would you describe your current feelings for Agent Walker?"

He gazed out the window at a gray sky. "The same as

last week. And the week before. I am interested in her romantically."

He looked back at her to catch her surprise. "You think I'm projecting affection because she saved my life."

"I'm making no such assessment."

"But it's possible."

"It's also possible that you do have a genuine romantic interest in her."

"She is intriguing to me. Very intriguing. I would like to learn more about her."

Eileen waited the same way his mother waited when she knew there was more. That patient, supportive gaze.

He said, "When I see her again, I'm going to ask her out."

"How does that make you feel?"

His smile faded. "I want to get to know her. I want to ask her out."

"But?"

A memory flashed. He had been with his mother in the old kitchen. A gangly teen, his voice had cracked. "I think I'm going to ask a girl out."

His mother had said, "Well, that sounds like something a boy your age should be doing."

"I'm not sure she likes me."

"That's a common fear."

"What if she doesn't like me?"

His mother had soothed his hand. "Romance is tricky. It's all about exploring the possibilities. Both sides have to want to be on that journey of exploration. I guarantee that you won't be the first or last man in the history of humanity to be rebuffed by a woman, and you will definitely survive it."

"But what if she *likes* me?"

His mother had smiled broadly "Ah, the infinite wisdom of my son who thinks too much. Why don't you see about getting to that first question before spending too much time on the second? What's her name?"

Eileen interrupted his introspection. "What are you thinking?"

It was as if a bowling ball had dropped against his guts. *I'm thinking about Mara.* Mara, the main role in the senior play. Mara, the class president. Mara, the soccer player. The girl that for an entire year had made him feel like he'd won the lottery. The girl who let him rest his arm around her shoulders in movie theaters. The girl who took his hand, showed him how to kiss, held him, opened him up to love. *Mara.* Standing on his front porch, telling him they were over. Her father had gotten a new job. They were moving. It was the easiest way.

Eileen asked, "Owen?"

Mara. The one that never came back.

Eileen asked, "Is this bringing back memories of perhaps another relationship?"

He gazed out the window and nodded.

"A past girlfriend?"

"My first."

"She broke your heart?"

"Oh, yeah."

"I can see that."

His voice tightened. "I've had other relationships."

"Ok."

"Finding women isn't a problem."

"Ok."

"The chase isn't where I have a problem."

"Ok. You are comfortable pursuing a romantic interest."

"Correct."

"But you think you have other problems?"

He rubbed the hair along the back of his head. "I'm not very good in relationships."

"How would you describe your history of long-term relationships?"

"Romantic?"

She smiled. "Yes. Of the romantic type."

"Not...not for a while. My mother says I have intimacy issues."

"Do you?"

"I think maybe. Yes."

"You ever talk it through with someone? Like your mother. She sounds like she's a good sounding board."

"Nope. She's tried."

"Anyone else?"

"Like a shrink?"

"Sure. Or a friend?"

"No."

She raised her eyebrows. "Something about Agent Domini Walker is stirring up some feelings. It sounds like feelings similar to what you had with that first girlfriend."

His jaw tingled.

"Well, maybe next time we'll dig into that a bit? What do you say?"

He shrugged.

She gave him a warm grin. "I suspect this Agent Domini Walker may be good for you, in the mental health sense."

Chapter Sixteen

The fourth floor of Javits was crowded and loud. Stepping from the elevator, Dom recognized Lea's head at the farthest desk, slightly away from the others, and moved quickly through the space.

Lea looked up. "The Collins case made the front pages of two of the Long Island newspapers."

Dom set down two coffee cups. "Huh."

"You're the shit."

"No names, right?"

"Oh, yeah. No names. Just that the FBI saved the day. But we all know you're the shit." Lea scooped up a coffee and made swift work of the pull tab. "Hey, I would have reckoned we would be taking the day off."

Dom sat in the side chair. "Yeah, sorry, you all right working?"

"Girl, you ring, I'm there. What have you got?"

"So, I went to see my father's old work friend."

"The retired guy in Brooklyn? Sure."

"Apparently, while in jail awaiting trial, my father said

something about dirty cops working in pairs. The exact quote was, 'Cops work in groups. Pairs. Two pairs. Always in these connected groups.'"

Lea pulled a face. "Cryptic but true."

"It got me thinking."

"Oh, I love that."

"You said his latest house is in Brentwood."

Lea punched the air over her head. "My research! Yes, ma'am, Brentwood. Home of the wealthy!" She side-eyed her. "What are you thinking?"

"If our theory is correct, Velk is taking bribes of some kind, or he wouldn't be able to afford the Brentwood home."

"Yes."

"Let's go really simple. Let's not complicate it. What would Velk have to offer in return for bribes?"

Lea leaned back and narrowed her eyes. "I see. Good question."

"What would the head of IA for law enforcement in the country's biggest cities have to sell?"

"All I can think of is dirty cops pay him to get them off."

Dom nodded. "I think that's right. And I think it's going to be that simple. I think that if we pull that thread long enough, somehow it will lead us back to before my father."

"Damn. I'm in."

"We can't go direct at Velk. Nothing full frontal."

Lea shook her head in agreement. "That cat is the smart kind of law enforcement."

"Agreed."

"So then how?"

"I think we have to work the edges. Find a thread at the outer edges. Any thread."

"Keep going."

"I say we don't start with the old stuff. We know he's probably *still* dirty. So, we pull outer threads that are happening now."

Lea wiggled her fingers in the air. "Oh, my lord, you seriously want to look at current shit. You are the queen. You are so bad ass."

"Maybe we can uncover something that's happening now. In the LAPD."

"Oh, praise black baby Jesus, I love it." Lea eyed her. "Wait…how we gonna investigate LAPD?"

Dom grinned.

Lea whispered, "Are you saying what I think you're saying?"

"I think I am."

"No!"

"Yup."

"You're going to LA?"

"Yup."

Lea pointed a finger at her. "You want eyes on him."

Dom nodded. "Oh, hells yeah, I do."

Lea rubbed her palms and cracked her knuckles over her keyboard. "So we need dirty LAPD who have gotten off in the last year or two."

"Exactly."

"We look for some kind of pattern or patterns."

"Exactly."

Lea nodded. "Oh, yeah. I like that."

Dom leaned back and sipped her coffee. "Now, how do we do that?"

"Oh, ye of little faith." Lea wobbled her head as she spun through the possible resources. "We can search news. We've got access to court records. Wait, I might be able to find access to LAPD records of misconduct. Oh, yeah, we can do this." She clicked her cheek. "After all this time working together, you still doubt me."

Dom was grinning.

Lea glared at her. "You just set me up. You know that I would figure out a way to dig into LAPD's dirty laundry."

Dom shrugged. "Maybe."

Lea squinted devilishly, as if preparing revenge. "Speaking of working together, I ran into Special Agent Owen Whyte yesterday."

Dom's heart fluttered. She remained cool. "Oh?"

Lea licked her lips. "He's looking good. I mean, you know how good he looks."

She's purposefully winding me up.

Lea said, "He said his shoulder is doing really well."

I shouldn't have teased her. "So that's good."

"He asked about you."

Keep it cool. "Uh-huh."

"I mean, he *really* asked about you."

She's coming in hard. Keep it cool. "Uh-huh."

"You gonna hit that or what?"

Dom's heart beat spiked. "Nope."

"What about romance? Maybe some potential heart strings there?"

"Nope."

"But something could be there."

"Nope."

"There *should* be something there."

"There isn't."

"Why not?"

"I don't shit where I eat."

"That idiom is overused."

Dom asked, "Is it?"

Lea nodded. "Yes. Yes, it is. How else we supposed to meet men?"

Dom sipped her coffee.

Lea placed her fingers back on the keyboard and looked determinedly at the screen. "He's a really good guy."

"Uh-huh."

"He really pushed me, asking what you were doing. So, I mentioned we were going to look into something."

In her chair, Dom stiffened.

"He guessed it was the Filthy Five."

Shame coursed through her veins. "What?"

Lea turned and held up a hand. "Hear me out. "

"No. I don't want him to know…about…"

"You can kiss that dream goodbye, girlfriend. He knows all about your shit. He didn't need no prompting from me. He's already done his homework."

Her mouth turned acidic and sour.

Lea twitched a finger. "Your family shit ain't that bad. You think it is, but it ain't."

Dom's stomach flipped.

"If I had to take a woman-who-studies-humanity guess, I'd even suggest he thinks your background makes you alluring. We're FBI. He's FBI. Yeah, FBI likes a mystery. They dig a challenge. And Domini Walker is a mystery wrapped in an enigma." Lea turned back to her screen. "Anyhoo, he's still on medical leave, so he has free time. He's looking into Velk's finances."

Dom wanted to throw up. "What?"

Lea turned to her. "I think he feels he owes you."

Dom's grip on her coffee tightened. "You had better be joking."

"Oh, no. Serious as a heart attack. But I can see why you might be upset."

"You got that right."

"Well, let me remind you that he's a forensic accountant. Apparently a very good one. His skills are exactly what we need if good ole Dartanian Velk turns out to be a corruption case."

Shit. It was a true statement. If this did end up a public corruption case, they'd need the paper trail, the receipts. But, shit she was pissed. Dom clamped her mouth shut.

Lea nodded. "See? Now you see. Swallow all that Walker pride and take his extra help. He's looking into a potentially bad guy from a money angle. That's all. He's not up in your skirts."

"I may kill you for this."

"Only cause you like him. If you didn't have the hots for him, you'd be taking that help lickity split. But we need his help so shush it."

Shit. Also true. Dom's heart clenched. "I may still kill you. Later."

Lea stuck out her chin. "Yeah, ok. I'll be here for that because by then he'll be up in your skirts."

Dom hissed, "Jesus Christ."

"Don't take the Lord's name in vain!"

You can't win. You can never win against Lea.

Lea turned to the screen. "Now, let's get truly distracted and see what we can find on LAPD misconduct."

Two hours later, they leaned back and stretched their backs.

Lea said, "So, that's a crap ton of complaints in one year. 3,544 is no joke."

"How do we pare that down, home in on any of those complaints that Velk may have had some hand in clearing?"

"Pare is the key word.

"Agreed. Let's drop this in an excel and tag them. And when I say 'let's' I mean you."

"Clearly. And clearly it's gonna be a long night."

Dom stood. "I'll get the coffee."

Lea's hands were already working the keyboard. "And a big block of that coffee cake, please. Big."

Chapter Seventeen

At 3 a.m. on the United red eye flight from LaGuardia to Los Angeles, with just over three hours remaining, the cabin lights were low and the passengers were quiet. Near the front of economy class, Dom sat looking out the window as sporadic groupings of lights from Midwest cities blinked in the darkness like fireflies. She pointed her toes to stretch tight muscles.

With every passing hour, she was closer to Velk and her nerves were on fire. She stared at the bright moon and imagined confronting Velk, with his dark eyes, high eyebrows, black hair, and thin chin. She would stand, feet apart, in his face. *I'm Stewart Walker's daughter and I'm here to redeem his honor.* What would he do? What would be his reaction?

The empty darkness surrounding the plane allowed her mind to wander beyond its normal constraints. She imagined him turning and fleeing. Or blinking in shock. Or smiling malevolently. Or denying any knowledge of her father.

The Glock in her shoulder holster pressed against her. She'd waved her credentials at TSA and they'd let her around the metal detector.

What if she drew her side arm, raised and sighted between Velk's eyes? Would it soothe her soul to know that she had scared him to his core with the threat of death? What if she actually pulled the trigger? Was it within her to actually pull that trigger?

Her father whispered, *"No, my Dom. That's not in you."*

Of course not. She knew she would never shoot Velk. For so many reasons. The Bureau. Beecher. Lea. Mila.

No, she'd end this legally, legitimately. Her job was to find Velk's crime against her father, get him indicted, get him jailed. From a seat in the courtroom, she would nod to him as he walked down the aisle in jailhouse orange. Dartanian Velk would know it was Domini Walker that nailed him.

She rolled her shoulders. They were nowhere near that day. This Los Angeles visit was only a fishing trip, likely the first of many. She and Lea were a long way from getting the evidence needed to lock Velk up.

Hours earlier, they had finished their first sorting of the 3,544 LAPD misconduct reports.

Lea had leaned back and reviewed their findings. "First grouping is police brutality and excessive force which is broken down in the following categories: baton beatings, choke holds, firearms, unlawful take downs, unlawful Taser, and denial of medical care. Next category is wrongful search and seizure. Then racial discrimination, abuse of authority, and neglect of duty. I've lumped together false arrest, forced confessions and wrongful imprisonment, and a whole other grouping that includes dishonesty, fraud, coercion. We've got the category of sexual assault and demanding sexual favors. And last but not least, we've got domestic altercations and drunk driving."

"Can you tell which complaints were brought by another officer? Internal complaints?"

Lea's fingers worked the mouse. "Yup."

"Those aren't the ones we're looking for, either."

"Ok. I'm screening out those 646. We've got 2,898 remaining."

"Let's get rid of anything that appears a one off. Like a domestic altercation or drunk driving."

Lea danced her fingers off the keyboard and read the screen. "We've got 2,060 remaining."

"What if we get rid of neglect of duty? That's passive. We're looking for crimes that were intentional."

"That's another 832 screened out. We're down to 1,228."

"Delete any officer that was a first-time offender. I'm thinking anyone who is connected enough to pay for clemency is probably a repeat offender."

Lea clacked the keyboard. "That leaves us 708 complaints."

"Does your list track those incidents caught on body video? It would be more difficult to exonerate something that's caught on tape."

"Ooooh, hold on." Clacking. "Yes! We're down to 339."

"Well, that's more manageable. Now screen out any that resulted in punishment, from a reprimand all the way up to a suspension."

"We've got 97 remaining." Lea leaned back.

"Of those 97 bad apples, if our theory is correct, some were cleared by Velk for a bribe." Dom entwined her fingers behind her head. "How on earth do we narrow those remaining?"

Lea stood and stretched. She strode a lap around the room.

Dom sipped her cold coffee and stared at the ceiling.

When Lea returned, she asked, "What did ole Roger say?"

"He said, 'Cops work in groups. Pairs. Two pairs. Always in these connected groups.'"

"So, of these 97, we're looking for cops that a) worked together at some point, b) that maybe went to school together, c) that grew up together in the same neighborhood, or d) any other connection."

"Can you do that?"

Lea cracked her knuckles. "Sure. You can find a needle in a haystack. You just have to pull out each strand of straw till you get to the ground and voila there, in the dirt, is your needle."

Later, as she was boarding the flight at LaGuardia, Dom had spoken with Beecher. "I'm heading to LA for two days."

"Wow. Velk?"

She had leaned over her feet to stretch the soreness along her spine. "We don't have anything solid. But you never do at the beginning."

"At the beginning. Wow. So, you're actually starting an investigation?"

"Unofficial, but yes, we're starting."

"Wow. What if you prove..."

"That Dad was innocent?"

"Exactly."

"That's the goal."

"Dom, do you *believe* he was innocent?"

In that moment, talking to Beecher, a heavy weight rose

from her shoulders, like a child's balloon caught in an updraft. Her eyes stung and she whispered, "Yes. I do."

He whispered in return, "Me too."

She swallowed. "Ok, just wanted you to know where this is going."

"Thanks for that. I love you."

"Love you, too."

Outside the plane's window, the patch of earth below was pitch-black. Dom leaned her head back and thought, *"I'll pull out every damn one of those 97 straws if I have to."*

Chapter Eighteen

The main room of the fourth floor of Javits was relatively empty. The morning surge of agents wouldn't happen for another few hours.

Lea dropped her bag on the chair by her desk, set her phone near the keyboard, and pressed the computer's power button. The familiar whir was loud against the quiet.

Dom wouldn't land in Los Angeles for three hours, which gave Lea an opportunity to research a new angle on the Filthy Five case. One had to be in the right headspace, and ideally in a quiet room, to read through legal proceedings. Research through the arcane details of court documents, trial transcripts, and witness statements took intense focus.

An hour earlier, an idea had begun to rankle. From earlier research into the case, Lea knew that three of the Filthy Five had been acquitted. In a far recess of her mind, she thought she remembered that those three had used the same lawyer while Antonio Belafonte had been defended by his brother and Stewart Walker had been represented by a small firm. Was there a reason the three exonerated police officers had chosen the firm Baker Kemper? Was Baker Kemper a potential crumb?

She straddled her chair and plugged in a search of court documents.

It only took one search to find the transcript of the trial against the three absolved officers and the name of their defense lawyer.

UNITED STATES DISTRICT COURT EASTERN DISTRICT OF NEW YORK
Transcript of Criminal Case against Robert Gessen, Art Dyson, and Mike Turner before the Honorable Clinton Reyes, United States Magistrate Judge
The Clerk called the court to order. Counsel for the defendants, Robert Pellum of Baker Kemper.

Lea smiled to herself. *Good morning, Mr. Pellum.*

One click later and she was scanning the Baker Kemper landing page, with its color image of a street scene below the gleaming One World Trade Center.

Baker Kemper. The trial lawyers of Baker Kemper have over 100 years of experience winning high-stakes cases around the country and across New York City. We continue to focus only on those small number of cases we know we can win and we devote staff and resources—from our talented lawyers through to our research staff—on behalf of our clients. We get outstanding wins.

She clicked on the photo of an older man with a soft chin and white hair.

Robert Pellum has a long history of working with the NYPD discipli-

nary system. He spent nearly 14 years as counsel to the Detectives, Lieutenants and Captains unions after leaving the Manhattan District Attorney's Office. He handles every case with the best representation that is not bound by allegiance to a boss, a union or an agency like the NYPD. His only loyalty is to his clients. During his tenure with Baker Kemper, Robert has represented NYPD, Corrections, Parole Officers, District Attorney Investigators and federal agents at all stages of the disciplinary process. He understands the weight and frustration of being accused of misconduct by Internal Affairs, CCRB, OIG, DOI, or another investigative group. He ensures that his clients get a fair treatment, regardless of wrongdoing. Every year since 2011, Robert has been recognized by Super Lawyers as one of the top criminal defense practitioners in the New York area. No matter what kind of trouble you are in, Robert is here to help.

Lea leaned back in her chair. That was one hell of a bio. Mr. Pellum literally advertised his expertise as a representative of the corrupt. *For a price, 'Robert is here to help.'*

She whispered, "One whose heart is corrupt does not prosper; one whose tongue is perverse falls into trouble. Proverbs 17:20."

She gazed at his pale blue eyes. *Oh, Mr. Pellum, how can I not delve into you?*

She clicked open a new tab, logged into Lexus Nexus, the legal data mining site, and pounced ten fingertips on the keyboard.

She constructed nine searches with a variety of keywords.

Robert Pellum had represented 2,368 cases since joining Baker Kemper twenty years ago.

She narrowed the cases with a single keyword: *NYPD*.

The system returned a list of 436 cases.

Lea picked up the phone and called four floors below.

An upbeat woman answered. "Library."

"Veronica?"

"Yup."

"It's Lea Peck."

"Hey. What can I do for you this early in the a.m.?"

"I'm gonna need a quiet space."

"Sure. When?"

"Now."

"For how long?"

Lea glanced to the screen. *436 cases.* "Could be awhile."

"Days?"

"Oh, yeah."

"No problem. I've got a cranium with no dibs on it."

Hidden in the back of the library were seven small study rooms affectionately referred to as craniums. SOS like Lea often used them for cerebral research. "Perfection. I owe you."

"Should I order boxes?"

The process of legal research involved the discarding of irrelevant documents, like chaff from the seed. "Oh, yes. Seriously, you're the best."

"No worries."

In Lexus Nexus, Lea clicked on the list of 436 cases and chose the tab, *"Print Related Documents."*

She stood, made her way to the vending machine bank to grab two empty cardboard boxes, and sauntered around the perimeter to the far corner. The smell of hot ink and singed paper hung in the space. The huge printer was already churning. Every five seconds, a new double-sided document dropped neatly into a tiered tray.

For free, Lea Peck, FBI Specialists in Research Proctology, is here to probe.

Chapter Nineteen

The clock read 7 a.m. and Mila had not yet heard Beecher, Tinks, or Dom. The thought was instantaneous. *Had Dom not come home?*

She wasn't anxious that she'd overslept. She had plenty of time before her first class for her orderly routine of coffee, shake, shower, and walk to the train station. But she *had* wanted to discuss the Inquirer photos with Dom over coffee. Now that would have to wait.

She rolled over and grabbed her phone. For the hundredth time, she opened the images she'd snapped and flipped through them. Many were of the crowd by the gravesite. The attendees were mostly males dressed in police uniform. They were older and appeared senior. That made sense, given Velk's status.

She wondered which of the guests were Naomi Cantor's family members? One of Virat's images, shot from a distance, had captured the hill, the mound, the open grave, the priest, and the rows of people. She pinched, slid and expanded on the tree at a distance from the crowd. Two men in dark coats stood close together under its shadows. Their features were fuzzy, giving them a sinister feel, like murderers watching the burial of someone they had offed.

She returned to the image of the two brothers by the gravesite. She pinched to zoom on a woman standing behind the right shoulder of the brother, Georgius. The distance between the woman and the nearest attendee gave the appearance that she was with the Velk brothers. The woman's face was partially covered by Georgius' shoulder, but Mila could tell the woman had long straight blond hair.

She closed the photo app and pulled up the cell number of Lea Peck.

Dom spoke highly of Lea and her big successes as a result of her dedication and intelligence. Someday, maybe Mila would be an agent that Dom spoke of warmly. She hit the call button and her heart spiked.

Lea answered, "Lea Peck."

Mila cleared her throat. "This is Mila Pascale."

A pause. "Uh, yes, hi, Mila."

"I may have found something."

"What are we talking about?"

"I was doing research." Should they speak openly about the cold Filthy Five case? Were FBI phones tapped?

"Mila, are you talking about what we discussed over breakfast on Saturday?"

Mila released her breath. "Yes, that."

"You aren't supposed to be working on that. Aren't you a student?"

"I'm at NYU. Criminal Justice."

"Like I said, a student."

Mila pushed. "I'm exploring tangentially-related topics. Additional color for your investigation."

"Don't use that word."

"Ok."

"Why are you calling me?"

"I have a question."

Lea sighed. "I'm kinda busy. Please, go ahead and ask it."

"It could be a something." Her voice sounded timid and it annoyed her. She tried to sound confident. "I would like to pull a thread."

"Damn, girl, get on with it."

"The suspect..." The term tripped up her train of thought. She rushed the words. "He was married. While he was in Philadelphia. The wife died. I got photos from the funeral. At the cemetery. Do you have tools to identify people in photos?"

Long silence.

Mila said softly, "Perhaps a long shot."

Lea replied, "But an interesting one. He was married?"

Mila exhaled. "Yes, six years. From his time in New York to his time in Philadelphia."

"Kids?"

"Not that I can find."

"Interesting."

Mila held her breath.

"The answer to your question is, yes, we have such tools at the Bureau. But I have to put in a request for each image. How many do you think warrant a request?"

"I believe one or two in the crowd of mourners."

Lea asked, "What do you intend to do once you have confirmed identities?"

Smart cookie. Dom was right about Lea Peck. Truthfully, Mila didn't have a plan. She hesitated.

Lea said, "You don't have a plan, do you?"

"No."

"If I put in those requests, you will discuss a plan with me?"

"I promise."

"You better, Missy. Because last time you went helping Boss-girl Dom you got yourself wrapped up with some nasty-ass cops."

Mila's heartbeat spiked. "Yes."

"You feel me?"

"Yes."

"If you find something, you call me immediately."

Mila said, "Yes."

"Because I'm doing you a solid."

"Yes."

Lea's voice softened. "I get it. Women gotta help women in this man's world. We're all stepping off the broad shoulders of those brave female warriors that came before us."

Mila straightened.

Lea continued, "If I can give a woman a hand, I will."

"Yes."

"But you're only doing research that is *tangentially*-related. That's it."

"Yes."

Lea's voice hardened. "Good. Because, Mila, let's be clear: as much as Our Father advocates forgiveness, if you go off half-cocked doing some Rambo-style bullshit and approach any individuals of interest, I won't see my way to help shit-ass-stupid a second time. Got it?"

"Understood."

"Ok, I'm gonna give you my email, you send the photos. Got a pen?"

Mila grabbed a chewed pen from the bedside table as Lea relayed an email address then hung up.

Mila quickly attached the two photos to an email and hit send.

She shoved off the bed and dressed hurriedly. No reason to waste time. Because while she and Lea had been talking, she realized there was, in fact, a new thread to pull.

In the photos, Mila hadn't recognized anyone except the Velk brothers. But she *had* realized that Aurélie Velk hadn't attended her sister-in-law's funeral. That was a very curious.

Chapter Twenty

The plane landed with three heavy bumps and the brakes screeched against tarmac. Cell phones came alive as chimes echoed across the cabin.

Dom turned her phone on and texted Beecher, *"Landed. Love you."*

As she was walking up the jet bridge, Lea called. "How was the flight?"

"Fine."

"I won't ask if you slept."

"Smart."

"I've pulled LAPD info where I can, and I've got lots of public civilian stuff. Of the ninety-seven bad apples, I've been able to chase down at least fifteen that have connections of some sort."

The LAX terminal was noisy. She pressed the phone to her ear and readjusted her backpack on her shoulder.

Lea continued. "One of them has more of those connections than the others. He went to high school with two other officers. He now lives within twenty miles of each. His kids go to school with another officer's kids."

"Ok?"

"And most importantly, he's got reports of misconduct going back ten years and he's never once been reprimanded."

"He sounds like a solid first needle in a haystack."

"Agreed."

"Ok, I'll take him."

"Name is Caleb Diehl. I'll send his home address. It's over an hour from LAX."

"I'm on him."

"I've sent your rental car info. Check your emails."

"Thanks." She moved down the ramp toward baggage claim. "If it's not Diehl, I'll come back out here and chase down all 96 other needles."

"Of course. But I like Diehl. He's as good a first start as any."

At the rental car reception desk, the young male attendant pulled up her reservation. "Oh, cool. You got the Tesla Model 6."

It meant nothing to her. "Uh-huh."

"You ever driven one?"

She shook her head.

"Cool. I'll meet you out front in five minutes. Show you the basics."

Twenty minutes later, she merged smoothly into the early morning traffic along Century Blvd and followed the GPS toward the California Interstate highway 405. The Tesla's console display map was clean and user-friendly. The wheel had a nice grip. Everything about the car was modern, almost futuristic.

As the rental car attendant had shown her, she pressed a button on the steering wheel and said, "Call Lea."

Lea answered in an instant. "So?"

Dom smiled. "A Tesla?"

"You on the highway yet?"

"I'm about to."

"Cool. Call me later." She hung up.

Dom took the curve onto the northbound 405 ramp and slid into traffic. She merged left to the fast lane.

The rental car attendant had plugged in the *Ludicrous* driving mode. "In this mode, this bad boy is the third fastest acceleration of any production car ever produced, beaten out only by LaFerrari and the Porsche 918 Spyder. But both those were limited runs." He winked. "You're gonna find out what 0-60 in 2.5 seconds feels like."

Ahead, an opening expanded and she pressed the gas. The car accelerated like a rocket. The force slammed her head against the headrest. The speedometer read 89 mph in an instant.

God bless Lea Peck. She laughed out loud. "Holy shit."

She lifted off the gas and returned to 70 mph.

By the Getty Museum, she put the car through its paces, weaving between others in the two fastest lanes. The car handled like a dream.

She followed the signs for 101 North and sailed through the long curve.

The traffic on the 101 North wasn't bad and she made the trip to Thousand Oaks in less than an hour. Palm trees lined the streets. Cruising through the neighborhood, she rolled down the windows. The lawns were tidy, the well-kept bungalow houses painted in earth tones, and the air smelled clean. The map displayed a huge gray area of parkland surrounding the residential streets.

Officer Caleb Diehl's house, one of five models in the community, was a single-story, one car garage with a brown front door. It was in the middle of a quiet, sleepy street.

She parked seven houses away, turned off the car, and called Lea.

The phone rang loudly through the interior of the car, and she lowered the volume.

Lea said, "Hi."

Dom stared at Diehl's house. "I'm here."

"Nice timing. How was the ride?"

Dom allowed a small grin. "This car is balls."

"A warrior queen needs some speed."

"And then some."

They sat quietly. After many stakeouts, they were comfortable in the silence.

Dom spoke first. "I wonder how much time this is gonna take."

"We have time. Nobody knows yet. We're just putting out fishing rods."

Dom said, "Driving up here, I wanted to veer off, check out his house in Brentwood."

"I hear you."

"I just want to run right at him."

"I feel that. But don't worry. We'll get him. We're on the case now. For the first time. And we've got some very smart ideas about how our man is messing around. We're gonna haul in those nets."

Dom chewed her lower lip. "You're right."

"Plus, righteousness and justice are the foundation of your throne. Psalm 89:14"

Dom laughed.

Lea insisted, "It's a skill, baby. Based on a whole shitload of bible study."

"Ok, I'll call you later."

From her backpack, Dom took out a dark blue baseball cap, slipped it low on her forehead, and pulled her ponytail through the back. It was tougher for witnesses to correctly ID someone if they hadn't witnessed the hair. She tugged out a bottled water and drank sparingly. Toilet breaks on a one-man stakeout were an issue. She couldn't lose sight of Diehl before he went into work, so there wouldn't be any bathroom breaks for a while.

The leaves on a nearby flowering bush fluttered and she wondered if the breeze was the Santa Ana's. For a fish out of water, she wondered how she knew that.

Chapter Twenty-One

Lea had gotten lucky. The library cranium room had a window and the morning sun splashed yellow across the long table covered in legal documents.

For the first hour, she'd made it through 40 of the 498 cases that Robert Pellum had tried in the US District Court of the Eastern District of New York. A box by her right foot was already almost full.

She stared at the remaining documents. This was going to take a while. She fished out a clean notebook and a new pen from her bag and lifted the next document.

United States Court of Appeals for the Second Circuit (Argued: March 2011)
Karem v State of New York
Published by New York State Law Reporting Bureau pursuant to Judiciary Law § 431.

John Karem's original 1999 arrest had been for possession. During his appeal, his lawyer, Jose Rodriguez, had argued the ruling based on the technicality: that the NYPD had falsely claimed to have had a warrant. During Karem's original trial, NYPD were not able to produce a warrant. In the appeal, Rodriguez claimed a conspiracy by the NYPD: in the first instance, that the NYPD had faked a warrant, and in the second, for their continued deception up to the original trial. Rodriguez claimed there had never been a warrant.

Lea rubbed her eyes. Why had her search for Robert Pellum yielded this document? What did Robert Pellum have to do with this case?

She began to skim the paragraphs.

The first reference for Robert Pellum was on page 26.

Jose Rodriguez: "We argue, your Honor, that the NYPD came looking for Karem specifically. We don't know why, but we do not believe it was for drug possession, as was laid out in the original trial. We have a particular interest in a lawyer on a separate case. A Mr. Robert Pellum of Baker Kemper—"

Judge Hammerstein: "That's quite enough. We are here today to review Mr. Karem's possession charge. I will not have you slandering members of the law profession who are not even involved in this particular case. Do we have an understanding, Mr. Ramirez?"

Jose Rodriguez: "Sir, we think it is relevant."

Judge Hammerstein: "I do not. Make sure that you don't do it again."

Lea sat back. Was this the only reference to Robert Pellum in the whole document? One instance? This must be a mistake.

Lea tapped the *Karem v State of New York* trial papers together and was about to drop them into the discard box when a hint of an idea rumbled her brain. She stared at the name John Karem. The hair on her heck quivered. John Karem.

She slowly set the document on the table and slid over her laptop.

Her fingers tingled as she opened the file titled *Research - Filthy Five in Court*. In the file were over thirty court documents she had uncovered and saved. She opened the one titled, *Stewart Walker August 27, 1999 transcripts*. At the top of the document, she typed in a keyword search for "*Karem.*"

On the screen, paragraphs and pages flew upwards as the curser sped to the bottom of the document and stopped to rest on page 195. The curser blinked alongside the name *John Karem*.

Lea whispered, "I knew it."

Page 195 was titled *List of Witnesses*.

Stewart Walker's lawyer had called for John Karem to be a witness in their defense. The lawyer had singled out the testimony of John Karem as important for his client.

She hit the search button again.

The cursor returned to the same spot on the page 195.

There was no other mention of John Karem. He had not testified. He had been called to court, but he had not appeared.

The skin at her hairline prickled.

She grabbed the John Karem appeal transcript and flipped to the front page. The original case number for Karem's first trial was *16-CV-4576*.

Slamming her fingers on the keyboard she pulled up Pacer and typed the case number.

John Karem, Plaintiff
Against
The City of New York
Defendants
August 27, 1999

Her eyes widened. August 27, 1999 was the same day as Stewart Walker's trial. Separately, on August 27, 1999, John Karem had gone to trial. On the same day.

What were the odds? She sat back; her fingers hovered over the keys. "Oh, Shit Almighty."

Someone had worked the system to prevent Karem's testimony. And only someone inside the legal establishment could have rigged the system.

Her right hand slapped the table. *So crooked. So very crooked.*

Chapter Twenty-Two

The smooth voice of a podcast narrator was murmuring about an elephant sanctuary in Kenya through the Tesla's surround sound when the door of Officer Diehl's garage slid open. Dom tapped the Tesla's display and the car went silent.

Inside the garage, bright taillights flashed as a white Ford 1-150 truck reversed. The truck's license plate was personalized and read *10-9867*. The 10 codes were used by law enforcement for the sake of brevity: 10-16 stood for domestic disturbance,10-4 for OK, 10-18 for quickly. Alongside the truck, in the second bay of the garage, peeked a cherry red back tail of a Porsche Panamera. Maybe surveilling Diehl hadn't been such a long shot.

The driver, a white male with dark sunglasses in a blue LAPD uniform shirt, backed the truck down the drive and Dom slid the lid of the baseball hat lower. Earlier, she had plugged in the location of Diehl's police station at 12312 Culver Blvd in Culver City, a neighborhood of LA not far from Santa Monica. Now, the Tesla's map showed the quickest route would take them through the coastal mountains of Malibu State Park and along the ocean on Route 1.

She let him turn off the street before she stepped on the gas. Even if she lost Diehl by a few car lengths as they traveled into the city, she'd be close on his tail.

The commuter traffic on the 101 heading south into the city was moving at a steady 75 mph. Dom stayed two car lengths behind in the fast lane. Only once did she fall behind, but the Tesla maneuvered easily through gaps in the traffic to make up the distance.

Twenty minutes later, the display map indicated for her to exit. Up ahead, Diehl also merged into the right lane. They both exited at Exit 22 toward Lost Hills Road onto Las Virgenes Rd and transitioned to Malibu Canyon Road that wound its way through a smattering of houses set in rolling hills of scrubby brush.

Thirty minutes later, Dom was two car lengths behind Diehl when they broke over the dry mountains and looked down on the sprawling green lawns of Pepperdine University. The chilled, salty air of the Pacific Ocean rushed through the car.

Ahead, Diehl cornered left onto Pacific Coast Highway just as the streetlight turned red. Dom slammed on the brakes as the phone rang through the car.

She rolled up the windows and answered, "Walker."

"Walker, it's Fontaine."

Oh, shit. She did not want him to know she was in Los Angeles. "Yes, sir."

"How you doing?"

The light turned green, and she punched the Tesla. "Fine, sir."

"I'm not asking what you're doing."

Diehl's truck came in view. "Ok."

"Listen, I got a call from the Bureau out in Long Island. They'll need some paperwork on the Edgar Collins case."

She slowed and slipped between a Mustang and a Saturn. "Ok."

"Can you get it over to them tomorrow?"

Waves rolled against a wide beach. "Does it have to be tomorrow?"

"No, I guess not. I'll tell them the day after?"

"Uh, ok. That should be fine."

"Good," he said and hung up.

After following Diehl's truck through the streets of Santa Monica, they arrived at the Pacific Community Police Station, a low-slung one-story brown building on the corner of Centinela Avenue. A bright American flag flapped in the ocean breeze. Brown grass and a low wall circled the building and two connected parking lots: one was designated for visitors, the other for *"LAPD Only."*

She circled the block and parked the Tesla on the side street.

From her backpack she pulled a green tie-dyed sweatshirt, huge sunglasses, and bright yellow running shoes. Both cops and crooks ID'ed law enforcement by their working shoes. She plugged earphones into her phone and called Lea.

Lea picked up quickly. "Hey, Fontaine's office was looking for you."

"Yeah. I talked to him."

Lea whistled. "It's so weird you're reporting to him. He's practically got you on fucking speed dial. What did he want?"

She exited from the car, softly closed the door, and strode toward the parking lot. "Some paperwork. I've gotta close out the Collins case."

"Huh. Did you tell him where you were?"

"No."

"You gonna?"

Dom reached the corner of the empty parking lot and caught sight of Diehl's truck among the personal vehicles. "No. Soon I'll be on a plane back to NY, no need to mention it."

"Where are you now?"

She scanned the back of the building for cameras and spotted one positioned over the lot. If someone were watching, they'd see her coming. She had to look like a pedestrian taking a shortcut through the lot. "I'm at Diehl's station. Can you stay on the line with me?"

"Sure. What ya gonna do?"

She jumped the low wall and walked with arms swinging in a relaxed fashion, eyes darting from license plate to license plate. "I'm gonna read license plates to you. Write them down. We'll need to track down vehicle owners."

"Roger."

She read the license of a blue, 1986 Corvette. "10-9854"

Lea said, "Copy."

Up ahead, a drab Ford SUV with a dent in the wheel had a plate that looked promising. As she approached, she could make out some of the numbers, but mud had splattered over most of the license plate. "Hold on, I'm gonna drop the phone."

She pretended to stumble, opened her fingers, and let the phone drop. As she leaned to grab the phone, she could make out the indentations of the plate's numbers. "10-4455."

"Copy. Does Diehl have a 10-license plate?"

Lea was a smart cookie. "Exactly."

"Nice. You want me to cross against our list of 97."

"Exactly."

She reached the end of the lot, circled up the back aisle and returned to the wall. "That's it. Just those two."

"Got it. This may take me a bit since we're talking dirty cops. I can't use NCIC." NCIC was the National Crime Information Center, law enforcement's electronic clearinghouse of crime data. "Let me call down to the LA DMV and throw some FBI weight around. I'll call you back."

Dom reached the Tesla and slid into the driver seat. "I'll be here."

Chapter Twenty-Three

Owen Whyte hadn't touched the brakes on the 2014 Triumph Phantom Black Bonneville since the Rahway Exit outside New York. With a flick of his wrist, he gassed the motorbike and felt it surge. The wheels tore up the New Jersey Turnpike.

The Triumph was a source of pride. He kept it under a top-of-the-line cover in a storage space in Jersey City that he could reach from Javits in one quick Path ride. Since the shooting, he'd been out twice to the small compartment with the loaded workstation to dabble with the multipoint sequential electronic fuel injection. The smooth acceleration proved that his handiwork had paid off: he was pleased with the results.

Earlier that day, he had searched public records for the Philadelphia properties of Dartanian Velk. The first had been purchased on July 1, 2003 and sold a year later on August 5, 2004. His eyes scanned the house's details.

Year Built 1930 (estimated)

Building Description3 STY STONE
Building ConditionAverage
Number of RoomsTotal of 12 rooms (4 bedrooms, 4 bathrooms)
Lot Size4,802 sq ft
Improvement Area3,573 sq ft
Frontage34 ft

Through the Multiple Listing Service, the bedrock of any real estate agent, he found that Velk had paid $710,000 for the property and sold it a year later for $945,000. That represented a significant increase in the home's value in only one year. It was an exceptional flip, but Velk could have used the mortgage terms to his advantage as the housing market was building to its peak.

Opening a new browser, he had looked up the address on a map. The house was within the city limits in a neighborhood near Philadelphia's famous art museum and the Schuylkill River. A street view showed a three-story townhouse with a broad stair and a red front door. It was a nice-looking place and a good-sized home for a senior police officer. But had it been worthy of the big payout on the flip?

He leaned back and stared at the photo. Given the market, the price he received for the sale of the home could have been legitimate.

But moving from $945,000 to a $3M Los Angeles home was a steep climb. Velk would have had to make an absolute killing on his second Philadelphia home.

Owen returned to the Multiple Listing Service site to track down Velk's second Philadelphia home. It was located in a suburb of the city called Penn Valley. The street view from the map showed a stately two-story Tudor with a curved driveway.

Secrets of the Angels

Year Built 1921
Building Description Single Family 2 Story Stone
Building Condition Good
Number of Rooms Total of 13 rooms (4 bedrooms, 3 bathrooms)
Lot Size 1 acre

Velk had purchased the home on August 8, 2004 for $990,000. He'd sold it March 2, 2008 for $2.7M.

Alarm bells pealed in Owen's mind.

It had been the weekend of March 14-18 that U.S. Treasury secretary Hank Paulson and Fed chairman Ben Bernanke had brokered a deal with JPMorgan to purchase Bear Stearns and bail out Wall Street. Foreclosures had littered the country. What were the odds that Velk had been able to close a deal just prior to that week that netted a roughly 270 percent increase on his home's value?

None. Owen's fingers slammed the keyboard. Ten minutes later, he found a login for Penn Valley's housing assessment records. In March of 2008, when the home sold for $2.7M, it had been valued at $1.5M.

Owen leaned back and stared at the screen. The only legitimate reason the value of the home could have jumped so significantly was an event in the neighborhood. Had something been built to bring up the home values? Had some development been completed? A new school? A new highway exit? It could be anything.

Owen had pushed back his chair, grabbed his coat, and head for the Path ride to Jersey City.

Two hours later, Owen slowed the Triumph at the bottom of the drive of a large Tudor house. Tall, old-growth trees lined the boundary of the property. A row of red and pink azalea bushes stood sentry under the three peaked roofs. A heavy dark door and wooden beams stood out against pale gray fieldstone walls. It was a rich man's suburban garrison.

He had spent thirty minutes slowly driving around the quiet, residential neighborhood. The homes were upscale and large. The lawns were well kept. A few mansions hid behind tall fences. But the tony elementary school that sat in the middle of four huge sports fields had been built in the 1950s. The nearest commercial area was two neighborhoods over and the nearest train station was twenty miles away. There was nothing about this neighborhood that would have increased the value of the homes in the middle of a global housing market crash.

Owen turned off the bike and slipped off his helmet. From a tall branch, a crow barked. The brisk air smelled like pine.

One of the most elusive ways to wash dirty money was to funnel it through real estate. It was a transaction between two people: the buyer picks up a clean asset, the seller walks away with cleaned cash. In most cases, no one notices.

Not this time.

Owen stared at the house as the conclusion solidified. In a years-long criminal enterprise, someone was lining the bank account of one of the country's most senior law enforcement officers by buying his properties at far above market rate.

Owen slipped his helmet back on.

The first question was, who?

The second question was, when did the relationship start?

Chapter Twenty-Four

Dom turned off the Tesla's radio and picked up the call from Lea. "Hit me."

Lea's voice boomed through the speakers. "First, sorry it took so long. DMV and all that. Second, neither of those 10-plates are owned by any of the 97 bad apples."

Damn. Damn. Damn.

"Dom, don't worry. This is just our first foray."

"I just don't like sitting and waiting."

"I hear that. How's it going?"

"You know. Surveillance."

"Fucking fun times, am I right? How's the ass?"

"Sore."

"Dom, I've been doing some digging." Lea brought her up to speed on the legal files. "I've got a splinter I'm going to pick."

Dom focused on the Pacific Community Police Station parking lot. "Good."

"What's your next move?"

She sighed. "I think I'll just have to continue with good old-fashioned tailing."

"Bet that car helps."

She cracked a small smile. "This car is pretty impressive."

"Fast?"

"Oh, *real* fast."

"Like racing fast?"

"It's got some serious chops."

"Hey, you know who else likes racing?"

The California sun beat down on the black asphalt of the empty parking lot. "Huh?"

"Owen Whyte."

Oh, Lord, Lea's at it again. Dom frowned and waited.

Lea said, "You know what else about Owen Whyte?"

"You're gonna tell me."

"You're fucking right I am. He's smart, that one."

"Uh-huh."

"What's the worst thing that could happen if you go out with him?"

Her heart spiked. "Shut it."

"Why? Cause you've foolishly decided you won't go out with that fine specimen of a man?"

"I'm not going out with him."

Through the car speakers, Lea's voice commanded, "Let me walk you through a nice, easy scenario."

Here we go.

Lea settled into the pace of a long story. "You two get drinks. Like a few drinks, you know, the amount that is required to loosen up two Type As. Cause you both are clearly not Type Bs, no matter how much you each think you are. But I digress. You two are sitting in a nice bar. And let's be clear. It's a nice bar. I'm not sending you two emotional popsicles to some cop dive bar, no matter how comfortable it is for you."

"You don't need to do this."

"That's true. But, as I was saying, you two are sitting there, talking about cases, cause that's what we do. You two are there, for at least an hour…"

Dom breathed in through her nose.

Lea's voice unexpectedly turned soft and sultry. "When Owen Whyte reaches over and places his hand on your knee."

Dom's heart leapt into her throat.

"He says something kind about you, gives you a compliment. Maybe, you've got great eyes. Or lips."

Dom held her breath.

"But you deflect. You try to change the subject. Cause you have that weird modesty."

How could such a young woman be so damn cutting? Dom swallowed.

"Finally, he tells you he knows all about your dad and it doesn't bother him. None of it bothers him."

The air stuck in her lungs and the vision of the parking lot went fuzzy.

"At this point, you down your drink. You know why? Because the singular defense you have against getting intimate with a man—or a woman, I'm not picky—is that you believe your family's past somehow makes you less than."

Lea Peck was a force to reckon with. "I wish you'd shut it."

Her sexy purr returned. "Then, at some point, cause he doesn't strike me as clumsy, lil ole hottie Owen Whyte is gonna reach over to hold your hand. Hmm, hmmm, hmmm. Those long fingers tangle up with yours. Your skin up that arm is gonna get all tingly."

Dom's stomach curled in a knot.

"Then, that fine chiseled face is gonna come in close. Those blue eyes, closer and closer. Our Lord can't help you now. Your boy's nose is about to bump yours."

Dom rubbed her eyelids and dropped her head. "Jesus."

"When his lips touch yours..." In an instant, Lea's tone turned neutral. "Nothing. No fireworks, no fire. Nada. Zero. Zip."

Dom's head popped up.

"That's the worst that could happen."

The sun was bright in the sky.

Lea continued, "Should you decide to go on a date with hottie Owen Whyte, the worst-case scenario is that there is zero chemistry. In that case, you two can proceed to be friends or colleagues or whatever. That's worst-case scenario. So, stop your imaginary resistance. We've had enough of that."

Dom leaned back. *Lea was a wonder. She'd pulled her all the way to here, mentally kicking and screaming. But she was right.*

Cars began filing out from the parking lot. It was shift change.

Lea chuckled. "But, Dear Warrior Dom, the more likely scenario is you two hit the romper room and blaze it up. Torch it. Wallpaper is scorched, ceiling gets smoked. Like the Towering Inferno. Cause then, well, then what are you two gonna do?" She laughed as she hung up.

Diehl's Ford truck exited the lot.

Chapter Twenty-Five

Mila jumped off her bike outside the Browning Gallery, a brick warehouse on W. 24th Street not far from the river, and locked it to a streetlamp. Hearing muddled but near voices, she glanced up and down the empty street noting only two parked cars: a tan Camry and a blue sedan. The hair on the back of her neck quivered. It was then that she noticed the High Line overhead and the flow of pedestrians.

She pushed through the wooden door and into the gallery's thick silence. Across four walls, massive colorful photos of landscapes were illuminated under bright spotlights. The floor, a shiny gray cement, also reflected the light. She quickly counted twenty-six bright bulbs overhead.

Walking past a snow-covered mountain under a blue sky and a prairie blazing in a burnt sunset, Mila felt soothingly small by the sheer expanse of the nature. By each image, a white card stuck to the wall showed them to be by the artist, Jose Manos.

The next room was half the size. The images were from

varying artists and styles. Four were oil paintings, seven were black and white photographs, and the far end displayed three intricate paper collages. She paused by a painting of yellow and white flowers against a brown background. The stems had been tightly packed into a green glass vase.

She entered quietly into the third room and an older gentleman with white hair behind a big clean desk looked up from his laptop. "Hi, welcome. Can I help you?"

She nodded and approached.

"I was wondering if I may see some work by an artist you represent?" She had practiced the line on the ride over.

He smiled gently. "Sure. Who would you like to see?"

"Aurélie Velk."

His face turned sad. "Oh."

She was immediately suspicious. "Is that a problem?"

"No…just…how did you hear about her?"

"I saw her work in a magazine."

He nodded as if that was all the answer he needed. "I see. Well, yes, of course. I'll just go get her work." He stood, but turned back. "Her work is exceptional. It's also a bit pricey."

Mila nodded. "That's ok. I'd still like to see it."

He smiled politely. "I'll be right back."

He returned with a stiff folder the size of a tabletop, set it down on the big desk, and gently lifted the top. "Unfortunately, art does tend to increase in value—"

A massive black and white image of an angel stood on a tall pedestal against a stormy sky.

Mila exclaimed, "Wow."

He shook his head. "Yes, well, I didn't realize that would be the first one. Sad."

What was he talking about? She looked at him.

"The angel," he said as if it explained.

"I'm sorry?"

His eyes widened. "I'm sorry, you don't know?"

Uh-oh.

"Aurélie Velk passed some time ago."

"She's dead?"

"Oh, yes. I'm very much afraid she is."

So much death. There was so much death around Dartanian Velk. "I didn't know that. When did she die?"

"Uhm, I feel like it was maybe ten years ago?" His eyes took in the photo. "Despite the uncanny subject of this particular photograph, Aurélie had a great talent. She could capture a moment with such clarity." He pointed to one of the dark clouds. "See that wisp there? You can almost feel the breeze that is making it whorl. She told me she took over fifty shots of this particular subject, and only one satisfied her." He gently turned over the photo, exposing a portrait of an old woman with gray, slightly frazzled hair and laughing eyes. "She did very good portraits, too."

"It looks like they've just shared a joke."

"That's a good observation. Aurélie had a way of pulling out emotions from her subjects." He turned over the photo.

Mila recognized the next image immediately. It was of Aurélie in a white button-down shirt, her dark hair cut in a short bob. Despite the reflection from the flash in her eyes, she was sad and unsmiling.

He said, "And that's a self-portrait of course."

She whispered, "She looks so sad."

"Well, yes, because she suffered so."

Mila leaned back to watch his face.

He frowned. "Well, with her depression. Oh, yes, she

struggled with it. Lots of artists do, but Aurélie really had a bad time of it. Of course, in the end, she lost her struggle."

Mila blinked.

He lowered his voice and nodded sadly before turning back to the portfolio. "She killed herself."

The next image was another black and white, this time of a small girl with long blond hair on a swing underneath a branched tree. The girl's head was thrown back and she was laughing as she squinted against the sun. "That's Lily, her daughter. She would have been eight or nine at that time. Sad to have lost her mother, especially since Aurélie was a single mom."

Mila's mouth dropped open and she leaned over the photo. *Aurélie had a daughter?* "How old would Lily be now?"

"In her young twenties, I would imagine."

It had to be the blond at the funeral, standing behind the Velk brothers.

Mila straightened as a thought trampled her mind. Had someone taken a photo of Jimmy at that age? Would he have been laughing? Tears stung her eyes and an inner voice pleaded, *If you want to come find me, Jimmy, I'll open my arms and hold you close. There is nothing that could have happened to you that would make me love you any less.* To silence the voice, she coughed and took a step back. With a deep breath, she said, "Uhm, thank you. I really appreciate you showing me her work."

"Of course." His tone said he recognized grief.

"I'd like to think about it."

"Of course. I absolutely understand. I'm here every day until three."

"Really, thank you, again."

Outside, she took a deep breath against the chill in her chest. Both the tan Camry and the blue sedan were gone, but she couldn't shake the feeling that someone was observing her movements. She stepped to the bike but watched the people on the High Line for a moment. No one was standing still. No one was looking down at her from above.

Chapter Twenty-Six

This time, Dom kept the Tesla tight on the white Ford truck, letting only two cars get between them. She did not know Diehl's destination and she couldn't afford to lose him.

From Santa Monica, the truck merged onto the 10 headed East into the sunset.

She pushed the Tesla tight and fast up the entrance curve and flipped down the visor as she merged into the right lane traffic. The skyline for downtown Los Angeles stood shiny against the pink sky.

Fifteen minutes later, as they passed over the octopus sprawl of exits for the 405, the traffic slowed to 30 mph. Out of an abundance of caution, she shot left into an opening and moved up on the bumper of the truck. The driver's window was cracked open two inches and white smoke billowed through. Fingertips held a cigarette near the glass.

She passed him.

He was again wearing the blue baseball hat and dark aviators. He did not glance at her.

For ten minutes, past pockets of gritty neighborhoods and blocks of Pep Boys and Collision Centers, she held the forward position. Slowly she made her way back behind the truck just as Diehl exited onto South Santa Fe Avenue.

Past storage units and block-wide parking lots, she kept a Honda minivan between them until Diehl sped through the yellow at the intersection of East 26th Street.

Ahead of her, the minivan stopped.

Damn.

Diehl's white truck receded down South La Brea Avenue.

The light turned green. The minivan didn't move.

Seriously?

Dom punched the horn for one quick shot.

The minivan lurched forward.

Dom shot to the left around the minivan.

Ahead, Diehl's truck was nowhere in sight.

Making a split decision, she cornered right onto 27th. The street was empty.

Damn it all.

Slowing, she glanced left and right in search of the white truck. On the right was a U-Haul facility. On the left, a small strip mall with two storefronts and an empty parking lot. Further on, a green fencing with razor wire circled a huge construction site.

There.

She lifted her foot off the gas pedal. Just inside the fence, alongside an office trailer, sat the white truck.

She exhaled.

Lea picked up on the first ring. "Talk to me."

"I'm outside a construction site." Dom relayed the address. Through the gate, a huge rectangular pit spanned the width of the block. Deep booms emanated from the hole as pylons were hammered into the ground. "Name on the fence says Universal Construction Co. Get what you can on them and whatever they're building here. Looks big, like a commercial building."

"Copy that."

Six cars were parked neatly to the left of the trailer alongside Diehl's truck. "My guess is Diehl's moonlighting as security."

"Roger."

On the far side of the gaping pit was a second parking of cars: a bulldozer, a crane, and two large dump trucks. "It looks like a legit operation. Big gear. Clean."

Lea said, "You're thinking maybe other bad apples also moonlight there?"

A dump truck rumbled past and turned into the front gate. "Maybe."

"If you're right, we could chase down that connection, cross tabulate against the misconduct that Velk cleared."

A security guard in a neon vest waved the dump truck into the lot. "Yes."

"But how do we ID any of the other 97 that work at Universal?"

Dom glanced over at the second gated entrance in the far corner where a second security guard stood sentry. "I don't know yet."

Five minutes later, a tan Honda whipped past the Tesla and cornered into the main entrance. The guard leaned toward the Honda's windshield, then waved the car through.

Dom's mind spun. The guard had peered at the windshield. He hadn't checked a clipboard. Something was on the windshield. She whispered, "A sticker."

Lea said, "What?"

"They're checking window stickers on the cars coming in. Diehl must have a sticker on his windshield."

"You could check against other stickers at his precinct station."

Dom said, "Exactly."

"But how do we know what the sticker looks like?"

"I'm gonna have to go inside, get a close-up."

"Didn't you just describe the fence and the security guys to me?"

"Yup."

"And the razor wire?"

Dom didn't have time to waste. "I'll have to find a way in when they shut down for the day. After dark."

Chapter Twenty-Seven

The offices of the law firm Baker Kemper were on Pearl Street near Water St. in the South Street Seaport Historic District. The address implied money. But the small conference room was shabby and dimly lit. As she set down her bag, Lea Peck thought, *I guess crooked cop lawyering don't pay like it used to.*

The door opened and Robert Pellum stepped through. He looked to be well over eighty years old and he limped his way around the table. His handshake was feeble. "Robert Pellum."

"Lea Peck, Federal Bureau of Investigation."

The collar of his suit was threadbare. "I was a bit shocked to get your call. I don't get many visitors from the FBI."

"Yes, sir."

He looked her over. "Are you an agent?"

"No, sir. I'm a Staff Operations Specialist. We provide research and case support to the analysts and agents."

"Yes, yes. Right. Well, please, have a seat." He shuffled

around the table to a seat directly opposite. "What can I do for you today?"

"I have been reviewing an old case—the Filthy Five—here in New York. The one where five—"

His look hardened. "I know the one."

"Yes, well, I've been looking into it in relation to a current investigation."

"Yes?"

"Yes, there may be some connections."

"How so?"

"I'm afraid I can't get into that, sir."

"Ok?"

"I have a few questions."

He watched her carefully. "Proceed."

"From what I can tell, you represented three of the five officers that were involved in the sting. Why did you not represent all of the accused?"

He looked to the ceiling. "As I remember, one of the two had a brother in the legal profession."

"Officer Belafonte."

"Yes, correct. So no need for him to use our services."

She smiled. "That makes sense."

"The other, I don't know about."

"Stewart Walker."

"Yes, that's right. I remember the name Walker now."

I bet you do, old man. "He was represented by a small firm."

"Oh?"

Why did she feel like he was *acting* the old forgetful man? "Yes, he was represented by a lawyer named Simon Bigg. Do you know him?"

"There are 180,000 lawyers in the state of New York, Miss."

She hated when she was called Miss. "Yes. That is true. Were the three officers you represented referred to you?"

He gave her a very confused look. "Perhaps."

She wasn't buying his ruse. "By whom?"

"Well, now, I'm not sure about that."

"Maybe the police union?"

"I'm sure I don't remember."

"Perhaps by Head of Internal Affairs Dartanian Velk?"

His eyebrows rose and old eyes were watching her sharply. "Perhaps. IA did make referrals to us. Over my career, I have worked on a number of NYPD cases. Mr. Velk and I crossed paths."

"But you can't be sure if Dartanian Velk referred the three Filthy Five officers to you?"

"Not that I can remember."

"Any ideas why Simon Bigg took on Stewart Walker as a client?"

"I'm sure he can tell you that."

"I'm afraid he can't," she said flatly.

His eyebrows rose again. "Ah. Well, no, I'm not sure why we didn't pick up Walker as a client." He rested gnarled hands on the table. "How is that pertinent to your current investigation?"

"I'm not at liberty, sir."

He shrugged as if indifferent, but his gaze was suspicious.

She said, "I've read the trial transcripts. You represented your three clients quite well."

His brows furrowed. "Thank you."

"You argued that your clients were only following orders. That none of them had been the ringleaders."

He shrugged again.

"That tact appeared to pay off."

"Yes.

"You argued that Stewart Walker was the one that organized the crime. That Walker came up with the plan in the spur of the moment, in the apartment, and instructed the others what to do. That he had, in fact, been the one to sit on the stolen goods in the warehouse while the other officers returned to their shifts."

"Yes?"

"All three of your clients testified to those facts. They were acquitted."

He watched her.

"It was a smart legal argument."

He crossed his arms.

"But I've read court transcripts from the separate Stewart Walker trial. Actually, I've read those transcripts quite a bit. That's what an SOS does. We are like rabid pit bulls—we don't let up. Simon Bigg should have pushed back on your argument. But he didn't."

"Ok?"

"While Walker was admittedly the smartest among them —that's clear in the transcripts—he was the most junior of the five. If I had been Walker's lawyer, I would have brought that up. The youngest, most junior of the five was calling the shots? That seems odd. Even unlikely."

"Unless, as you say, he was clearly the brightest."

"Even then. It just seems odd."

"Well, I didn't follow the Walker case or trial."

"But you knew he got convicted?"

"Yes, well, I suppose I did see that in the news."

Lea leaned back. "And he killed himself in jail, not much later."

"I did not know that." But his face lied. Pellum was lying.

"See, Simon Bigg argued that Walker was set up, that he, and the others, were entrapped."

Pellum waited.

"It obviously wasn't a good line of defense. It didn't work with the judge. Mostly because Bigg didn't have any evidence of entrapment."

"Miss Peck, I've given you quite a bit of my time, and I'm not sure, at this point, where you are going with this."

"Well, in reading the transcripts, I've started to wonder if maybe Simon Bigg wasn't too concerned with the outcome of that trial. It almost seemed like he was going through the motions, but not really giving Walker solid representation."

"Miss Peck, I do have other things I need to get to today. Other than whatever this expedition is."

"In reading what happened in the courtroom, if feels like Bigg knew Walker had a get-out-of-jail free pass. As if he had some secret weapon." She splayed her long fingers across the scratched wood conference table. "But in the end, his secret weapon never materialized, and Stewart Walker went to jail."

Pellum didn't say a word and his gaze was hard.

"There was one witness on the defense list. His name was John Karem. He never showed up for the trial—"

Pellum rose. "We're done here, Miss Peck."

"John Karem went to trial for another offense on the exact same day as Stewart Walker. What are the odds of that?"

He waved a palm toward the door. "Now, Miss Peck."

Karem was the key.

She rose, nodded, and strode from the cheap old dusty room.

Chapter Twenty-Eight

Owen Whyte stepped to the counter of the next available clerk for the Brooklyn City Register Office, a skinny white guy with a goatee, and laid his FBI credentials on the counter.

Twenty minutes earlier, he had circled the cobble streets of Dumbo in Brooklyn before slowly rolling the Triumph down a ramp into a parking structure. He parked the motorcycle by the elevator lobby, slapped down the kickstand, and turned off the engine. As he took the stairs two steps at a time to the first floor, he yanked off his helmet and strode into the lobby.

The goatee guy's eyes widened, but only slightly. City clerks were beaten down by a thankless job. "How can I help?"

Owen said, "I would love some help tracking down some property titles."

"Sure."

"All I've got is a name. I need a reverse search. Likely more than one residential going back in the nineties."

The goatee guy hovered his skinny fingers over a grubby keyboard. "I'm ready."

"Dartanian Velk." Owen spelled out the last name.

The clerk gave no look of recognition as he typed in the name and waited for the results. "Yes, there are some files. It looks like we've only got hard copies. Give me ten minutes, maybe more."

"That's great. I'll wait here."

Ten minutes later, Owen sat on the outside stoop of the building. Across the street, the air brakes whined as a panel truck inched into a tight parking spot. He slipped four sheaves of paper from the manila envelope the clerk had handed him. The first was a backwards chronological listing of Velk's three New York properties and any related legal actions. Owen focused on the dates, the home values, and their addresses.

RECORD DEED OWNER: Velk, Dartanian
PROPERTY ADDRESS: 376 East Eight, ST. PROSPECT PARK SOUTH, BROOKLYN
DEED DATE: 7/18/2003
PARCEL # 398675930585678
GRANTOR: Velk, Dartanian
MORTGAGE INFORMATION: Wells Fargo
MORTGAGE NAME: Spartan, LLC, Brooklyn
MORTGAGE AMOUNT: $999,000

RECORD DEED OWNER: Velk, Dartanian
PROPERTY ADDRESS: 378 Ocean Parkway, KENNSINGTON, BROOKLYN
DEED DATE: 7/18/1999
PARCEL # 398675930585678
GRANTOR: Velk, Dartanian

MORTGAGE INFORMATION: Wells Fargo
MORTGAGE NAME: Ios, LLC, Brooklyn
MORTGAGE AMOUNT: $750,000

RECORD DEED OWNER: Velk, Dartanian
PROPERTY ADDRESS: 2158 63rd Street, BENSONHURST, BROOKLYN
DEED DATE: 12/5/1997
PARCEL # 0695847556969
GRANTOR: Velk, Dartanian
BUYER: Bosporan, LLC, Brooklyn
AMOUNT: $378,000

Velk had owned and sold three properties in Brooklyn between 1997 and 2003, the period before he moved to Philadelphia. With each sale, he'd made a tidy profit and was able to move to a nicer neighborhood, getting closer with every move to the top area around Park Slope. This was normal as careers and income rose.

Three atypical things stood out from the summary. First, the buyer of Velk's first property paid in cash. There was no bank mortgage listed. Second, none of the owners were individuals, they were all business. Finally, all three businesses had Greek island names.

Owen's neck tingled. *Who uses the name of Greek islands?*

Across the street, the name splashed across the truck was *Henry's Painting.*

"Exactly," he mumbled. *Had related businesses, who wanted to hide their identity, bought all of Velk's properties?*

The driver of the panel truck stepped down from the driver side.

Owen slipped the sheets back in the envelope and pulled out his phone. He searched for the most recent buyer, Spartan, LLC, Brooklyn in the Dun and Bradstreet. The site listed fifteen employees and revenue of $10M.

It took Owen three more searches, squinting at the small screen against the glare of the sun, to determine that Spartan, LLC was represented by Bondar Partners, a law firm.

Next, he repeated the search for the 1999 buyer, *Ios, LLC, Brooklyn. Ios* listed twenty people and revenue of $21M. It was also represented by Bondar Partners.

The third search for Bosporan, LLC, now closed, had also been represented by Bondar Partners.

"Bingo," he mumbled. Front companies were used by any number of individuals, not all of them criminal. But only criminals bought off law enforcement officials.

Across the street, the driver returned, unlocked his door and hefted himself into the cab.

Owen pulled up a map and plugged in *Spartan Venture, Ios,* and *Bondar Partners*.

Three dots splashed on the screen. All within four blocks of each other. In Brighton Beach.

The truck started up with a belch and pulled from the space.

Brighton Beach.

Owen watched the truck retreat in the distance.

Brighton Beach was Ukrainian mob territory.

Owen slid on his helmet.

Chapter Twenty-Nine

John Karem lived near the Langston Hughes housing projects in the Brownsville neighborhood of Brooklyn. It was one of the most unsafe neighborhoods in all of New York. Lea Peck had arranged to meet him at a diner after work. She was finishing her first coffee when a 6'3" broad-shouldered black man stepped through the front door.

She gave him a nod.

He dropped his weight in the booth opposite.

"Thanks for coming, John. I really appreciate it. I appreciate you."

He nodded.

"You want something to eat? On the Bureau."

"Nah, just a coffee is good."

They flagged a waitress and waited for his coffee.

He rubbed his face. "You say someone's digging into an old case?"

"The Filthy Five."

He nodded heavily. "I knew it. I knew when you called it was about that case."

"A family member wants to find out what really happened."

"And this family?"

"Also Fed. One of them is Fed."

"You know him?"

"It's a she. And, yes, I work with her. She's righteous."

He settled against the booth as if to tell a story he didn't tell often. "I got done in, back then."

"For what?"

"First time for possession. Cocaine. I didn't do no crack. Just hustled cocaine. Not big time. Side money. My old friend was a dealer. He let me have a side hustle. Just me and him. No gang. Nothing like that."

"That's what they busted you for?"

"Yup."

"How long were you in?"

"Five years. I got early parole. I got my GED up there. Used that dang library. Read a lot. After I got out, got my life back on track. Moved on. You know?"

She nodded.

"But when I got done in, even my court appointed lawyer knew it was wrong. He said it was fishy."

She leaned on the table. "How so?"

"I didn't understand it at the time. I mean, lots of my friends had been sent up so I didn't think too much about. I was too scared. But then when I'm in jail, I was thinking about it a lot. It was weird how they busted me. Came at me. Intentional. Planned. Said they had me under surveillance" He shook his head. "Weird. I wasn't nobody. Small time. They found my normal baggie. At the time, I thought they were gonna squeeze me for info on my friend. I told my lawyer that, that surely they were gonna lean on me to rat out my friend."

"What happened?"

"They never offered me a deal. Nothing. Then the judge came in, sentenced me, and away I went. You know how it is, all them black boys waiting to get sent away. Nobody cares."

She asked, "What do you think now?"

He sipped from the mug and gazed out over the busy street. "I'm no genius. I was never a smart kid. I work for a living, I don't use my brain, you know? But when you're sitting in jail, you got all the time in the world. And you got lots of other guys to talk to. Everybody got a story. What my lawyer said, it rung around in my head. Target. He said, 'they targeted you'. That stuck, you know. Why they wanna target me? I ain't nothing."

"Did you figure out why?"

He nodded. "I knew when you called that I'd be telling this story. It's got its own life. It was gonna come out no matter how long I never said nuthin'."

She held her breath.

He rolled his shoulders. "That was back when they called it Alphabet City. They didn't call it all Lower East Side or LES some shit like they do now. Like it is some hot property. Back then, it was Alphabet City. Nothing great. I used to work maintenance on some rental buildings down there. For some asshole property manager. That's a shit job. They don't pay you for nuthin' and you're always on call cause there is always something going wrong with those buildings cause they old and they don't put no upkeep money in them. I mean, why would they? They squeezing blood from a stone with them old buildings. No new pipes, no new electric. But, hell, who cares, you know? They get them renters. Always getting renters. Anywhere on the island, they got space, they can rent it. Crazy."

Lea waited patiently.

"So, I'm working maintenance. I'm at this one particular building all day, trying to fix a window grate on the first-floor back. Cause it opens to the alley. A long thin alley. Mostly for trash back then. We didna have no recyclin' back then. Just trash and rats. Always fightin' them big-ass rats."

She smiled at him.

"So, I've got my toolbox out, sitting on one of them trashcans, and I've got this damn heavy window grate sitting up against the wall. And I'm about to prop it up—hard for one cat—but I need to put it up against there so I can go inside and screw it in. One too many fools breaking in at night, rummaging through the basement. I mean, that alley is empty and dark at night." He rubbed his eyes. "Anyway, I'm fixin' to push it in when this dude comes down the alley. He's clearly 5-0. I remember looking up, seeing him, and knowing he's a cop right away. So, I lower that grate back to the ground. It's heavy. And I didn't know what this copper is gonna do. I put my hands up by my chest, show him I'm no threat."

She nodded. "Was he in uniform?"

"Oh, no."

"So undercover?"

"Yeah. He in street clothes. But was 5-0." He clicked his cheek, a shorthand signal for *damn straight*.

"White?"

"Back then, they almost all white." He continued, "But he ain't looking at me. He was counting windows." He pointed up, as if to an imaginary building's second floor. "He was trying to figure out what particular building he wanted. You have to count down the alley, count the windows in the buildings. There ain't no street numbers back in that alley."

She waited.

"I had my work overalls on. I mean, he sized me up quick. I mean, a big black dude doing maintenance isn't such a big deal." He shook his head. "Nah, he didn't pay me no mind. I nodded to him all 'Hello, Mister.' He kept walking. He stopped two buildings down."

"And then what?"

"He walked up to the door and tried to open it. But it was locked. I mean they all locked back there."

"And then?"

"He stood there for a long while. Then he left."

She swallowed. "Later, upstate, you figured this incident was important?"

Karem finished his coffee and set the mug down on the table with both hands. "This FBI lady you work with, you say she's good?"

"The best. Straight up."

"What's her name?"

"Domini Walker."

He nodded, as if that fact helped make a decision for him. "That white undercover 5-0 that came looking at that building that day, he was one of them Filthy Five that got busted two days later. After they stole product and cash. From that building."

The implications dropped like dominoes. One of the Filthy Five was at the scene two days before the crime. He was there early, setting up the sting.

She blinked.

Karem gave her a sad smile. "Yeah, you see it now, dontcha? Just like I eventually saw it, too."

She gasped. "He was setting up the crime scene. He was in on the NYPD Internal Affairs sting. At least one of the five was a mole for NYPD Internal Affairs."

Karem sat back, as if the load on his shoulders had been lightened. "I didn't know it then, but I figured it out later."

"You could have ID'ed him."

He pointed at her. "Exactly. There you go, my sister."

"They didn't want you to testify. So instead, they imprisoned you."

His whole upper body swayed with his nod. "I also figured out that Stewart Walker's court date and mine were the same."

"Lord Almighty in the heaven."

"Ain't that right?" He nodded. "They didn't want me to testify at Walker's trial."

"Because the officer you saw wasn't Walker."

"Exactly. It was the only thing that made sense. They needed to send Walker away. Blame it all on him. They musta had it out for him. They wanted him out of the way."

They had it out for him. They wanted him out of the way. She rubbed her forehead.

He clicked again as he shook his head. "Dirty cops. Dirty cops and their dirty games. Fishy. Just like my lawyer said it was."

Do not be frightened, and do not be dismayed, for the LORD your God is with you wherever you go. "John, do you know who you saw in that alley?"

"I spent five years inside. I know all their names. And you definitely don't never forget the one that did you in."

She swallowed.

He spat the name. "Officer Robert Gessen."

She shook her head in sympathy. "Oh, my Lord."

He stood, said, "Thanks for the coffee."

She rose swiftly. "John, thank you. Thank you."

He nodded. "I expect this will come back at me if your girl wants to chase it. I'll testify. This time, I'll testify. You tell Walker's daughter, I'll do it for her."

Chapter Thirty

Dom's eyes stung, her mind was foggy, and her scalp itched from the dry airplane air.

It had been late, almost 7 p.m., when most of the workers at the Universal Construction site had climbed into cars and pulled from the two parking lots. The security guard at the far rear exit was the last to leave in a run-down Subaru and he loosely locked the gate with a padlock on a long hanging chain.

But it wasn't until 9 p.m. that the guard at the front gate crossed the fifty feet to the trailer and stepped inside. A few minutes later, he hopped on a moped, drove from the lot, and closed but did not lock the front gate.

Only Diehl's truck remained.

Overhead, the city's lights cast against a darkening night. She pulled up the hood of her black sweatshirt, tightened it around her face, and slipped from the Tesla.

The pit beyond the weak trailer light was an ominous pitch-black.

She jogged to the front gate and stood in the shadows

for a beat. The street was empty. She took hold of the one side of the gate. If metal screeched against cement as she swung it open, she would have to find another way in.

But the gate opened smoothly, and she slipped inside. If Diehl emerged from the trailer, she would be standing starkly in the empty lot.

She inhaled deeply, leaned forward, and sprinted toward the truck.

Forty feet, thirty, twenty, ten, five.

She skidded to a stop by the driver's side door and dropped into a crouch. A passing car's high beams swung across the lot, but the shadows of the trailer remained dark.

She popped her head up. The light in the trailer was still on.

She slipped out her cell phone and snapped three photos of the driver side window.

By touch, she stepped around the front bumper to the passenger side. The beam of light from the trailer window cast light across her back.

She lowered her profile against the truck. Holding up her right hand, she snapped four photos of this side of the windshield.

Inside the trailer, the light snapped off.

She slipped the phone into her jeans pocket and dropped to her knees.

The door of the trailer opened.

She dropped to her chest, her nose an inch from the cement.

Heavy feet clamped down wood stairs.

She placed her hands over her face and rolled under the truck.

Boots crunched around the end of the trailer.

She stopped rolling, facedown. The back of her hands pressed against cement.

Footfalls crunched alongside the driver's side.

She clamped her lips tightly.

The driver's side door opened and the interior light beamed across the lot.

She held her breath.

The truck shifted as Diehl settled in.

She squeezed her eyes as the engine roared to life, the deafening noise rattling her chest. She pressed her palms tighter to her face.

Cement crunched under tires as the truck reversed in a wide arch. The beam of the headlights swung toward the fence and then the gate.

She rolled quickly back to the shadows at the foot of the trailer.

Diehl stepped from the truck to open the gate, drove through, then returned to lock the gate with the padlock and chain. A minute later, the lights of the truck disappeared down E. 26th Ave.

Dom stood and dusted cement dust and gravel from her palms. Her bones ached. Her knees pounded from hitting the pavement. Limping, she reached the gate.

At least she had the photo of the windshield and whatever sticker was there. If she could match that against one or more of the other 97, they would know Universal was the connection and this trip, the hours of surveillance, and the nighttime incursion, would all have been worth it. They would have their first lead.

Diehl had double looped the chain. She yanked on the nearest side of the gate: there was no give. She would not be able to squeeze through.

The razor wire on the top of the fence coiled the length of the lot. There was no way over.

Slowly, she turned.

The pit yawned in the dark, a black mouth to hell.

There was enough of an edge to make it around the perimeter.

She leaned into a slow jog on wobbly knees.

Reaching the pit, she broke right, staying close to the gate. Running along the rim, her imagination ran high on adrenaline and lack of sleep. She imagined slithering monsters writhing at the bottom of the pit while ghosts rode hot gusts from hell.

Reaching the far parking lot, she leaned over her knees and gasped in full lungs.

The double gate this side did not have razor wire. She jammed her toe into the wire, climbed over, and dropped to the sidewalk on the other side.

Chapter Thirty-One

Dom pulled into a McDonald's drive-through and ordered two Big Macs and a water. It had been eight hours since she'd eaten the last of the provisions from her backpack. She parked behind the building and wolfed down the first hamburger while she opened up the photos of Diehl's truck. Despite the darkness of the Universal Construction lot, the camera had captured a clear image of the left side windshield and a green sticker. The logo for the company was a crane in flight high above a round earth.

"Gotcha," she whispered.

Her mind was mush. After thirty-six hours without sleep, her memory, reason, and decision-making would be impaired, and she would have delayed reaction times. She desperately needed to sleep. Instead, she put the Tesla in drive. *Almost there.*

Twenty minutes later, she approached the staff parking lot of the Pacific Community Police Station on Centinela Avenue. The neighborhood was extremely quiet. There were only twenty cars parked for the few officers working night shift.

She moved slowly down the aisle between cars and scanned the windshields. The first nine windshields were clean.

What if she had been wrong to chase this lead? Her heart fluttered against her ribs. *Stick with the plan.*

The Universal Construction sticker appeared on the upper left corner of the windshield of a black Jeep. She sprinted to the rear of the Jeep and snapped three images of the license plate. Now would not be the time to get sloppy. She knelt in the shadows and checked the images were legible. The photos were clear. "Gotcha."

The next sticker was on the last car in the aisle, a 1980s Mercedes sedan.

Two staffers plus Diehl made three LAPD officers working security for a private company. Three was not a coincidence. It was a pattern.

She raced around to the dented bumper, crouched by the license plate and snapped three more, checking the images on the phone. The photos were clean.

She pivoted and jogged across the parking lot. The light from the streetlights seemed to waver and oscillate. She blinked heavily to clear her eyes.

Sliding into the driver's seat, she said, "Call Lea," and shut the door.

Lea's voice boomed over the car's audio. "Talk to me. What did you find?"

"I've got two more license plates. They also have Universal stickers."

"Girl, you are a warrior! Hit me."

Dom read the plates and as redundancy, fumbled to send the images to Lea via text.

"Got 'em. I'll run them."

A curtain of exhaustion fell behind Dom's eyes. "This makes sense right? This angle? Is this making sense to you?"

"In all the time I've worked with you, you've made reliably correct decisions. Every single time. It's fine, Dom."

Her head was heavy and she blinked against the still wavering streetlights. "Lea, I need to nail him."

"You eat anything?"

Lea's voice came to her muffled, as if under a wave. "I got McDonalds."

"You still ok to drive?"

"Yes, barely."

"I've got you a room at the Holiday Inn one mile from your location. It's got Tesla charging. Go get some hours in the rack."

The urge to close her eyes was overwhelming. "Yes. Roger that."

"Get some sleep." Lea dropped her voice. "Don't worry. You're gonna get him."

The hotel room faced the interior of the block and Dom wondered through a haze if Lea had specifically requested a quiet room. The carpet was made up of colorful circles, rings upon overlapping rings. They appeared to spin independently at different tempos.

She fell facedown across the bed and was asleep instantly.

Part IV

*only when dawn comes tiptoeingtip-toeing
ushered by a suave wind,
and dreams disintegrate
like breath shapes in frosty air,*

—Lola Ridge, "Secrets"

Chapter Thirty-Two

KIEV, UKRAINE

A brass bell chimed as Police Officer Ionna Moroz pushed into the small resale store. The smell of dust and oil from a leaky furnace floated in the air.

A wizened man with a shock of white hair and thick glasses looked up from behind a wooden desk. "May I help you?" he creaked.

If Ionna wanted to be insulting, she would call this a high-end pawnshop. But she was not here to judge. She was here to follow some leads as a moonlighting detective.

She approached the desk. "I wonder if you can help me. I'm trying to figure out where a couple things were purchased. And since you buy things…I thought maybe you'd have some informed thoughts."

He spread his hands as if to say, "go ahead."

She pulled out her phone, pulled up the image of the gold angel pendant, and showed him. "Any thoughts on this?"

His arthritic fingers took the phone. "Custom. Likely made right here in the city. The craftsmanship is ok, not notable. I'd stick with local artists. Maybe try over at the jewelry bazaar behind Besarabsky Market."

The mention of the big food hall made her stomach growl. She had not eaten since the two slices of toast seven hours earlier.

She leaned over him and flipped to the image of the gold bars. "And these."

He held the phone to his thick glasses. "That's a very nice size bullion. Too rich for me. Most of the time, you can order this over the internet." A gnarled finger pointed at the stamp. "This is PAMP. From Switzerland. Lady Fortuna series. These sized bars are really for investors. Not much for collectors. One of the leading manufacturers. Also, big names are Credit Suisse. The US one now is called Asahi, but we don't buy from them much. And of course, the one out of Australia, Perth Mint. You'll want to take this over to Hymie's on Yevhena Konovaltsia St."

"Thank you."

Ionna, the successful detective, strode from the building.

Two hours later, a young man met her in the front room of Hymie's Gold.

She showed him the photo of the gold bars. "I would like to confirm the provenance of some gold bars."

"Yes, of course. Follow me." A mechanical lock clicked and he led her through a side door.

As she followed him into a smaller back room, she said, "Someone told me these sized bars are mostly bought by investors."

"Yes, that's true. The manufacturers, in this case PAMP Suisse, usually sell them in bulk. Not always, but that is their intent. They tend to sell them as close to the value of the melted gold as possible." From behind a tall table, he held out his hand for her phone and examined the photo.

"You're lucky, because PAMP now uses some remarkably interesting technology called Veriscan that will tell you the provenance of the bar and where it was purchased. If this is legitimate, I should be able to tell you the actual owner. I'll be right back."

A few minutes later, he returned with a printout. "The bar in your photo was purchased last year by a woman named Aneta Omelchenko."

"Yes."

"She purchased it from here, in fact."

"From here?"

"Yes. Coincidentally. According to our records, she ordered one or two bouillon a year."

"She ordered every year? For how many years?"

"The most recent five were in our system. I had to look up the other thirty-five's serial numbers. They weren't in the app yet. Both PAMP and we keep very precise records. It's important when you deal in precious metals. Turns out, Ms. Omelchenko purchased all the bars here. One or two a year. Starting in 1997."

According to her sister, Aneta Omelchenko had been modeling overseas from 1996 to 1998. "Are you sure?"

"Oh, yes." He pointed to the printout. "Every year since 1997, she bought them on the same day, December 28."

It was the same date on the *Kyiv Post* newspaper.

Ionna rode Syretsko-Pecherska Line to the Palats Sportu station and strode past the green marble walls under the bright lights in the peaked central hall ceilings and through the crowds. She exited onto Velyka Vasylkivska St, past the fancy stores, the luxury shopping mall Mandarin Plaza, and into the Besarabsky Market, as instructed by the pawnshop owner.

Inside the large market, the crowds filed past stalls where middle-aged ladies smiled.

Ionna picked up a bag of dried mixed fruit and munched as she walked through the cavernous area.

Out the back, she cut down the small block and entered a long, narrow building. Lined up along the sides of the main aisle were small cabinets that at this time of day were opened displaying pottery, hand knitted wares, and a variety of jewelry.

She paused at a cabinet that displayed jewelry similar to the gold angel pendant.

A young woman smiled broadly. "Yes, *Pani*?"

"I'm actually trying to track down something. I wonder if you can help?"

"I can try."

Ionna pulled up the image. "Do you have any idea who could have made this?"

The woman leaned over and moved in close. "Huh. No. I've never seen that before."

"Do you think anyone in here could help me?"

"The woman at the first stall, she's been around forever. Maybe she knows. Careful, she can be cranky."

The old woman at the front stall had huge breasts underneath a black cotton blouse and long curly gray hair. She eyed the photo of the pendant and nodded. "Yes, yes. I remember those. Haven't seen them around in a long time."

Ionna waited.

"The girls back in the day used to wear them. At the old club."

"What club?"

"The old Black and White club. I worked in a shop next door."

"The girls from there? The waitresses, you mean?"

The old lady smirked. "That's cute."

"I'm not trying to be cute."

"No, *Pani*, they weren't waitresses."

Color poured into the mystery, fleshing it out. "Call girls?"

"Whatever you choose to call them."

"What did you call them back then?"

"Hostesses."

The colors were dark and sinister. "What did they do?"

"What you'd expect. Spend time with the men who came in."

In a flash, the mystery filled in. Aneta Omelchenko hadn't gone overseas from 1996 to 1998 as she'd told her family. She had been a call girl at a club called the Black and White. "Did the girls live back there?"

"You're a smart one, aren't ya?" She nodded.

"Who owned the club?"

"But you're gonna need to be smarter than that, my dear."

The old lady would not touch that subject because it meant organized crime. This was Kiev. Not all things had changed with the revolution.

Ionna changed tact. "So, the girls from the old Black and White club wore these necklaces?"

The old lady eyed her. "Not all of them."

"Which ones?"

"Ones that had to take some time out."

The colors of this mystery were shades of dark. "How long was that time out?"

"Now you're catching on."

Long enough for a pregnancy? "A few months?"

"Yes."

"And when they returned, they had these pendants?"

"Yes."

Aneta Omelchenko had fallen pregnant, had carried the child to term, and had returned bearing the angel pendant of a mother. "Did the club owners know?"

"The owners didn't give a shit, dear *Pani*. We're talking disposable women."

"I understand."

"I think you do. Now, I need to get back to work."

"What was the address of the old Black and White club?"

"It was just around the corner. Down the block from the Ludwig Hospital."

Chapter Thirty-Three

Through the third floor Bobst Library window, lower Manhattan's skyline rose against a bright blue sky. The sun cast off a few scattered clouds.

The keywords *Lily Velk* had turned up in only one hit on the internet and Mila clicked open the *Psychological Bulletin* article.

Maternal Depression on Child Behavior Problems: Supports the depression-distortion hypothesis
Dr. Rebecca Buchanan
Research output: Contribution to journal › Article › peer-review
Keywords: Women's health, mother-child interaction, infant development

Abstract: Maternal depression has been described as leading to a significant presentation of behavior problems in children. This study evaluates this "depression-distortion" hypothesis. Survey data from mothers, teachers, and fathers, was further tested against self-reporting from youths between the ages of 10 and 14 years. Findings supported some validity of children subjects externalizing and internalizing maternal depression. Particularly illuminating was the difference in daughters internalizing their moods. This is the first in a series projects.

Mila would have missed the Lily Velk reference had it not been for her habit of skimming footnotes and endnotes —both are important—at the end of the article. Lily Velk appeared as a research assistant to Rebecca Buchanan, a professor at NYU.

Mila returned to her search and pulled up the NYU Psych Department site. She clicked on a photo of Professor Buchanan, an unsmiling woman with a square face under an unflattering haircut, and read the bio.

Education:
M.S., Ph.D., The University of Chicago, Department of Biological Sciences
M.S., Notre Dame University, Department of Biological Sciences
Areas of Research: Temperament/Parenting, Developmental Psychopathology, and Cross-cultural Differences
Dr. Buchanan has made significant discoveries on the development of early temperament programming in infants. Her research focuses on individual preferences for auditory and perception among infants leads to preferences or aversions later in life. Her seminal work has been reference in preeminent projects with the World Health Organization. Dr. Buchanan was the 2016 recipient of the Harlan Award, an annual award for outstanding achievement in the developmental psychopathology.

The abstract of a related article caught her attention.

Maternal Behavior Predicts Infant Neurophysiological and Behavioral Attention Processes in the First Year

Rebecca Buchanan, New York University
New York University
Keywords: infancy, EEG predictive, maternal behavior
Abstract: This study examined the development of neurophysiological and social processes in the first two years. Tests on EEG power change in medial frontal and interactions between mother and infant at 5, 10, 15, and 20 months. The working hypothesis was that the infant's ability to control attention helps regulate emotional reactivity which can lead to more socially appropriate behavior in childhood and that early caregiving has a strong correspondence to infant's appropriate regulatory capabilities. The contrary argument that delay in development of attention and related ability to regulate will likely predict maladaptive and poor regulatory skills.

Mila skimmed the thirty-page tome, dense with technical words, neural synchrony, higher-order cognitive abilities, neurocognitive networks, and midfrontal cortex. Much of the substance was lost on her, but she understood that the professor had been testing brain activity against mother and infant interactions to predict child development. Was brain activity determined by the relationship between the mother and infant? What happened to a child's ability to trust when raised in a state of adversity?

To Mila, the experiment was unnerving in a Nazi-lab kind of way.

She sat back and stared at the screen. Lily Velk must have come to NYU to prepare for a career that was born from deep personal wounds. The motivation was very similar to Mila's except she had chosen Criminal Justice.

Mila looked up the location of the School of Psychology's library. It was two blocks away.

She jammed her laptop in her bag and headed for the door.

A black male student with a big afro manned the Information Desk in the inner lobby. He looked up as Mila's shoes tapped across the linoleum. "Can I help you?"

Mila swallowed. She had decided an authentic approach was better than botching at deception. "Uhm, I'm currently an undergraduate here. I'm interested in learning about the Graduate program in Psychology." None of those were lies.

"Ok?"

For an information desk person, he wasn't very friendly. "Well, I'm a bit OCD. I like to do my homework." Also, not lies.

"Ok?"

"Is there any way I can get access to the library so I can read some resources?"

"Sure. I can get you a visitor's pass for a week. You can use the library resources, including the portal. The portal has class curriculum, primary research. We do a lot of virtual, also. Almost every class is recorded. Does that work?"

That was better. She nodded.

"What's your name and student ID?"

She provided them.

"Mila Pascale. Yes. Criminal Justice. Undergrad." His fingers punched the keyboard. He nodded over his shoulder to the inner room. "You're in. One week. Just use your ID."

Her heart raced. That wasn't nearly as bad as it could have been.

An hour later, she discovered Lily had recorded Professor Buchanan's classes. The video was set in the corner of a small room with ten students around a long table. Professor Buchanan sat at the head behind a laptop with thick, black rimmed glasses.

Buchanan kicked off the class "Let's start with a review of the study we discussed on Monday. Jamie, do you want to give us a brief synopsis?"

A girl with bright purple hair read from a notebook. "The study is looking at infant temperament. The parent is the one doing the reporting via an ongoing questionnaire. These are filled out every week at agreed upon hours. This is done by both primary and secondary parents. Subjects..." she looked up, "...I still hate that they use that. I mean we're talking about babies."

Exactly, Mila thought.

Purple Hair Girl returned to her notes. "Subjects were from the age of three to six months in the first phase. Then six to nine. Results: older infants received higher scores on Approach, Vocal Reactivity, High Intensity Pleasure, Activity, Perceptual Sensitivity, Distress to Limitations, and Fear. The little ones were higher for Low Intensity Pleasure, Cuddliness/Affiliation, and Duration of Orienting. Interestingly, male infants obtained higher scores on Activity and High Intensity Pleasure, and female infants were rated higher on the Fear scale."

Buchanan nodded. "Great. Thanks for that, Jamie. So, we're just getting into clinical with infants and I want to check in with you all. I know this can be uncomfortable. Lab work on humans in general is hard at first, hard to remain objective. With infants it is even more so. So, let's get a temperature gauge on how each of you are doing."

Mila tapped up the volume on the video.

One by one, the students around the table shared their feelings.

A slim Asian guy said, "It's all about science. We're here because we believe in the science. I'm ok with that. I didn't think I would be. You know, you hear about these classes on campus and you wonder how you're gonna feel, and I didn't know how I would feel. But it turns out I'm ok."

Buchanan asked, "Do you think, Sonny, are you comfortable with the reading we did on the protocols and ethics? Was it enough for you?"

Skinny Asian Sonny shrugged. "Yeah. It was helpful to see both sides. So, yeah."

The next student was a tiny woman with spiked dark hair. "I actually did some additional reading. I wanted to know if there were any legal actions over the years about studies on infants."

Buchanan grinned. "That's great, Anne, just great. What did you find?"

"This and that." Spiked Hair Anne also shrugged. "But in the end, I'm like Sonny, I'm ok. I wasn't sure, either, but now I'm ok."

Blond Lily Velk was next in line.

Mila paused the video.

Lily's poker straight hair fell from a middle part close to her hollow cheeks. Her lips were tight. She had thin shoulders under a white shirt.

Mila hit *play*.

In the video, Lily said, "I'm ok. But just only."

Buchanan asked, "Do you want to expand?"

"Well, it's a little close to home, this work with infants..."

The room was silent.

Lily took a deep breath. "I was adopted. Things about the adoption haunted my mother her whole life. She never spoke about the process. I always wondered if it was because she felt she had lost out on that early bonding." She frowned. "But my mother had bigger issues also."

Buchanan said, "That's brave of you to share, Lily.

Thank you. Mother/infant relationships are so fraught with externalities. How do you feel proceeding with this current topic in our studies?"

Lily's brow furrowed. "I'm glad we're getting deeper into the science and the findings. I broached my personal issues in a paper last semester in Psych 2012. I fleshed out some of the residual psychological resistance I have. I'm hoping that the objectivity of the work this semester will help me understand that."

Mila jotted down *Psych 2012*

On the screen, Buchanan said gently, "So far, you feeling comfortable?"

Lily nodded. "Yes. So far."

"Let's all agree we'll check in with Lily over the course of this term with compassion and empathy."

Around the room, heads nodded.

Mila stopped the video.

Twenty minutes later, Mila had found a copy of the report Lily had mentioned in the digital resources of the library. She pulled up a copy of the study titled *Personal values influencing a psychiatrist's professional judgment for Psychology 2012 Physiological Basis of Behavior* and skimmed the contents. The report read like a reference guide with reviews of articles and academic sources.

There were no firsthand revelations made by Lily.

But in the footnotes, Mila found gold.

Lily had referenced a brochure from an adoption agency called Hope for Children.

Mila exited the search, closed the laptop, and slid it in her bag with a sense of conclusion.

Always read the endnotes and footnotes.

Chapter Thirty-Four

Owen Whyte sank into the gratifyingly soft cushions of the armchair in the gently lit basement office of the Chelsea townhome.

Eileen Bremmer gave him a gentle smile. "Good to see you."

"You, too."

"How's the shoulder?"

He grinned. "Not top of mind."

"Ah, good. You look…enthusiastic about something."

"I am."

"Want to tell me about it?"

"I probably shouldn't."

Her eyes narrowed. "Because you're doing work when you are still officially on inactive duty?"

"Something like that."

"What goes on in this room, stays here."

"I don't want to get you in trouble."

"Why don't you let me worry about that?"

"You sound like my mother."

"I'll take that as a compliment."

He laughed. "Yeah, you should."

She gave him a grin. "So, what's going on?"

He brought her up to speed on the Dom investigation and his own discoveries. He did not tell her the name of the suspect.

She said, "Well, that does sound very interesting. I'm glad to see you engaged in work related topics. It can get boring sitting around."

"Yes!"

She gave him a knowing grin. "So you've been working alongside Special Agent Domini Walker?"

"Actually, no. She's on the West Coast. I'm working with her teammate. But all the findings are getting coordinated."

"That's exciting."

"It is. Nice to have something to chew on."

"How about your feelings for Ms. Walker?"

"They are still there."

"So that's promising."

"And increasing."

She raised an eyebrow. "Ok."

"I'm definitely going to ask her out when the timing is right."

"And how do you feel about that?"

"Nervous."

"Didn't your mother tell you a long time ago that was healthy emotion, given the circumstances?"

Owen pursed his lips. "Yup. That's exactly what she said."

"But…"

"I still feel nervous. And it doesn't feel healthy."

"I can assure you; it is."

He leaned back into the chair. "It helped."

"What's that?"

"To talk to you about it. About the nerves."

"So that's good. Tell me more."

He examined the ceiling. "I'm acknowledging that she makes me nervous. I'm letting it just be a feeling. You know? Like I'm not trying to push past it."

She waited with the calm of a therapist.

"It's not as terrifying as I thought it would be."

She nodded.

"The lessons I learned from that first girlfriend..." *Mara.* "They don't seem so bad now. Somehow they lost their... weight."

"That's good."

He gave her a chagrined half smile. "I sound adult. I sound like I'm an adult."

"You do."

"Huh. Any advice?"

"What did your mother say about relationships and both people?"

"Both sides have to want to be on that journey of exploration."

"I think your mother is wise."

He acknowledged the truth with a grimace. "Yeah."

"What does that exploration look like to you?"

"Learning, time together." He shrugged. "Quiet time."

"There you go. That acknowledgment and the interest to move forward is good." She clasped her hands. "Feelings that come from abandonment can linger. For a long time. Especially if it happens at a formative point, say, in the teen years."

A bowling ball sank against his guts. He hadn't used the word abandonment, but that's the emotion conjured up by the Mara experience.

She continued. "Now here's the adult perspective. Only children can be abandoned. Only children are left truly helpless. Fully functioning adults aren't left helpless. They move on."

His mind began spinning. "I'll take that concept away with me. To digest."

Her gaze never left him.

"So the anxiety is worth the risk?"

"That's one way to look at it."

So many thoughts. Too many thoughts. It had been easier without the professional clarity of a therapists. "Thanks. I think."

"You are very welcome."

Chapter Thirty-Five

In the dream, the pressure in Dom's ears produced a deep baritone hum that rattled in tiny pulses against the bones of her skull. She tried to ignore it as she groped for the sandy bank of a large pool of greasy water. Her fingers stretched toward the shore, but the water was thick like oatmeal. The ooze was pulling at her waist, moving up her chest as she sank. It was quicksand. She was in a pool of quicksand. A white ghost appeared on the shoreline. Behind him, tall thin trees spiked against a roiling sky. The phantom circled the pit, translucent and gauzy.

She tried to swim against the sludge, but it only pulled her deeper.

A glow emerged around the ghost, lighting up his face. It was Dartanian Velk.

At his feet, a Glock lay in the sand. Her fingers clawed across the surface of the muck, grasping for the gun.

From the tree line, a man emerged, walking slowly toward the ghost of Velk. It was Owen. He raised an arm. In his hand was a gun. He took aim at the ghost and a gunshot ripped through the air. The ghost vanished. Dom screamed, "No! He's mine! That shot is mine!"

She woke covered in sweat.

Next to her, on the pillow, her cell phone was vibrating. She smashed the call open.

Lea said, "Dom, it's Lea."

Dom's voice came out groggy, scratchy. "Hi."

"I need you awake."

Dom sat up and scanned the room for a coffee maker. It was on the refrigerator near the closet. "Give me five."

Five minutes later, Dom called back. "Ok. Go."

"I'm gonna bring you up to speed. I'm putting you on speaker. I've got Owen here—"

Her heart fluttered and she sat on the edge of the bed.

The sound of space opened up in her ear.

Owen said, "Hi, Dom."

She swallowed, said, "Hi."

Lea broke in. "Owen, you go first."

His voice was deeper than she remembered. "Velk has made exceptional profit buying and selling his homes." He described the sales of Velk's two houses in Philly before LA. "I then went backwards. Got hold of his real estate deals here in New York. Same pattern. Sells at a significant markup."

The coffee was working. Her brain was firing. "He's laundering his payoffs."

Lea said, "Exactly."

Owen said, "I got the records of the buyers of his New York homes. Shell companies named Spartan, Ios, and Bosporan?"

Dom said, "Bosporan was an ancient Greek city near Odessa. Ukraine."

That gave him pause. "Yes. That's correct. All three

front companies are represented by a dodgy little law office name Bondar Partners. In Brighton Beach."

Dom said, "Brighton Beach?"

Lea was quick. "Exactly."

"Are we talking Ukrainian mob?" Dom stared at the wall.

The phone line was silent.

Lea said, "There's more. Owen, tell her…"

"Universal Construction, while based in LA, is owned by a shell company we think has roots in New York."

Dom spoke the conclusion out loud. "Dartanian Velk is owned by the Ukrainian mob."

Owen said, "For a long time. Perhaps his whole career."

Lea said, "Dom, there's more."

"Go."

Lea continued, "I was digging around in legal documents. I found something."

"I'm ready."

Lea asked softly, "You sure?"

"Yes."

"I met with a guy who was at the Lower East Side site two days before the 1999 sting. He was doing some work at an apartment over on 5th Street."

"Uh-oh."

Lea insisted, "This eyewitness is solid. His story is good."

"Tell me."

"He saw Officer Gessen staking out the building. Two days before."

Time stopped.

Lea said, "Gessen was in on the sting. He was the mole for Velk."

The jigsaw pieces fell together. Stewart Walker was

homing in on Velk's corruption. Velk had to get rid of him so he organized a sting, used inside men, and they all sent Stewart away.

The coffee roared back up her throat. She leaned over and fell to her knees. Bile shot across the circles in the carpet. Her eyes blurred from the tears and the swirls in the carpet circled in on themselves. It was impossible to know where the pattern started or ended.

She remained over her knees taking in deep breaths.

In her ear, Lea's voice was soft. "We have the last piece. I found the lawyer who represented the three NYPD officers that got off. It was the plan…"

"To make my father the fall guy."

Lea's voice was a whisper across the phone line, "Yes."

Dom stood and caught her reflection in the mirror. Her hair was in knots and her runny eyes were circled in dark. But the person staring back was the same as always.

Stewart Walker's voice whispered, *"I told you. You're that good, my Dom. You're that good."*

She closed her eyes against the sting. *They'd solved the mystery.*

Lea broke the heavy silence. "Dom, we have all the pieces."

Owen said, "The Bureau will open an investigation. This is more than enough."

Lea said, "We have enough. Dom, you can come home."

Dom snapped open her eyes. "No. We don't have enough. We need incontrovertible proof. When they open an investigation, I want the evidence against him unassailable."

Lea said, "I hear you."

Owen said, "So do I."

Dom whispered, "This isn't over yet. We need more."

Lea said, "Ok, we'll keep digging. But it is time for you to come home. We have plenty enough to dig from here."

Dom wiped her mouth. "Before I fly back, I want eyes on him. I just want him in my sights. In person."

Lea said, "I get that."

Owen said, "So do I."

Chapter Thirty-Six

In the hills of Brentwood above the busy thoroughfare of San Vincente, Dom had parked on the quiet street of Hanley Place down the street from the walls of Dartanian Velk's home.

Earlier, she'd asked Lea to put in a request for any cell phone ID pinging from this address. Across the open phone line, she asked, "You got the request in?"

Lea said, "Yes, I'm pulling them up on a map." Keys clacked. "Yeah, I got him. He's there at his house. Wait. There are two cell phones pinging from his house."

"Two?"

"Yeah, maybe a girlfriend."

"Or maybe a burner."

"Agreed. Just so you know, there's a five-minute delay on those pings. It's not instantaneous."

"Copy."

"Also, don't miss your flight."

Dom glanced at the car's clock. 7 a.m. The flight didn't leave until 10. She had her backpack beside her and her service Glock under the driver seat. "I'm good to go. I've got a bit more time here."

Owen asked, "How's his Brentwood place?"

"Big. Behind a wall. Some kind of modern Mediterranean. Orange tiled roofs, adobe walls. A silver Range Rover in the drive." She stared at the gate and the very nice house. It would have been lovely to live in such a nice house. Go to a private school, play sports, not have secrets to hide.

She wasn't unhappy with her life. It was just that some things would have been better if they had been different. So much easier.

All these years, she had thought Stewart Walker had let her down, abandoned them. But he hadn't. He had seen corruption at the highest levels, and he had decided to take it on. One might even call him a hero.

Both Owen and Lea must have been looking at the house online, because Owen said, "Oh, yeah. Nice place. That fits his M.O."

Lea asked, "Where you parked?"

"At the corner. It's super quiet up here and nobody parks on the street."

"That's Los Angeles for ya."

They sat in silence, before Lea said, "Hey, you know what, you broke this case. You didn't let up. You never gave up. Your determination got us to this point."

Dom blew out her lungs.

"Let us not grow weary of doing good, for in due season we will reap, if we do not give up. Galatians 6:9"

Dom smiled.

"Did I make ya smile?"

"Yup."

Another five minutes passed before Lea asked, "You mad?"

"Oh, yeah."

"Cause you can't go after that motherfucker yourself?"

"Exactly."

Lea said, "You think you can catch him on his way to work?"

"That's my objective."

"Just a look—"

"I know, I know. I'm not going to approach him. No matter how much I want to." Her fingers clenched the wheel. "I wish there was a smoking gun. I'm nervous whoever gets the case won't have enough to indict him."

Owen said, "I hear that, Dom. But I think we have a lot to get this opened."

Lea chimed in, "Owen, here, has done some good digging. We've already got receipts."

The line went silent again.

Owen was turning out to be a big asset.

The scenario Lea had composed earlier, of the bar and the kiss, now sent a flush up her cheeks. The last time she'd slept with someone, it had been Len. They'd gone on two dates. Their third round of sex had been tender and after, he had pulled her close to his chest. She had cried. Len had acted like he hadn't felt the tears dropping on his bare skin, but she knew he had. In the end, she had called it off. There was no way he could handle her job.

She swallowed. "Owen, thank you." The thought of crying on Owen's bare skin made her cringe.

Owen's voice was soft. "You don't have to thank me."

"Anyway, thanks."

Owen said, "Of course."

Lea broke in. "You talked to Fontaine yet?"

"I'll call him now."

Fontaine picked up from his executive assistant. "Walker."

"You said I should reach out to you first."

"I'm listening."

It took a full five minutes to fill him in.

When she finished, he said, "That's quite a theory, Walker."

A cricket chirped outside the car. "I realize that."

"You're opening a lot of worms."

"Yes."

"A fucking can of vipers."

"Yes."

He groused. "You don't do anything by half, do you, Walker?"

"I'd have to agree with that, sir."

He said, "For starters, if this goes anywhere, this can't be your case. It has conflict of interest all over it."

"Yes, sir."

"Where are you now?"

A subconscious antenna tickled her brain. "Outside Velk's house in Los Angeles."

His anger flared. "You what? Are you kidding?"

At the end of the street, there was movement. "No, sir."

He snapped, "At a distance?"

From the left of the intersection, the front bumper of a car inched forward. It was a sports car. A red sports car. "Yes."

He snarled, "Walker, what are you doing at his house?"

She hesitated, said, "I think I needed to get near him." *After all these years.*

Fontaine quieted. Special Agents had their own ways of chasing the bad guys.

The car pulled slowly across the intersection. It was a red Porsche Panamera.

He asked, "When is your flight back?"

The hair on her neck prickled. "In a few hours."

The Porsche stopped in the middle of the intersection.

Fontaine said, "Ok. Come find me when you get back. We're going to take this off your hands."

Dom squeezed the Tesla's steering wheel to maintain calm.

Fontaine pressed, "You hear me? This is not your case. Get on that plane."

Inside the Porsche, the driver wore a dark baseball hat and dark sunglasses. He looked down Hanley Place for a long moment. At her.

She said, "Yes, sir."

The line went dead.

The Porsche punched out of the intersection.

The driver had been Officer Diehl.

Chapter Thirty-Seven

The adoption agency, Hope for Children, was located in a tall office building in Kips Bay, just before the corner of East 28th Street on 3rd Avenue.

Mila's bike ride uptown had taken twenty minutes. The traffic along 1st Avenue by Stuyvesant was hairy and she had worked her way over to 3rd. At 24th Street, she noticed her back tire was soft and made a mental note to stop at the bike shop near Madison Square Park on the way home.

In the small lobby, a kind black security guard in a rent-a-cop uniform smiled as she approached.

She said, "Hope for Children."

He slid her the sign-in book and handed her a pen. Looking at his watch, he said, "2:36"

She signed, "*Nancy Drew, 2:36, Hope for Children.*"

He nodded toward the elevators behind him. "16th Floor."

In the elevator, she considered the possibility that Hope for Children was a red herring, a nothing burger. It absolutely could be. There wasn't a lot to go on, other than Lily

Velk had sourced it in a graduate school paper. But an investigator could not always tell what a significant lead would be.

She wondered how many times Dom had walked into an office, flashed a badge, and began asking questions. How many of those times had she unearthed something new? It was the job of FBI agents to chase down leads regardless of guaranteed success.

The elevator pinged on the 16th floor, and she stepped into a silent hallway. Metallic name plates identified the offices behind black doors. Along the hallway, Hope for Children was the fifth door.

Mila took a deep breath and pushed inside.

Brightly colored poster sized photos of happy children plastered the walls. Underneath, empty chairs were lined up like a doctor's waiting room. The only person in the room was a middle-aged Latina woman with dark hair pulled back. From behind a counter, the woman smiled widely in an understanding, sympathetic way. "Can I help you, my dear?"

The woman thought she was there because she was pregnant with an unwanted child. In that instant, Mila knew the persona she would take. She let the door close behind her and stepped toward the counter.

The woman pointed to the one of two chairs in front of the counter. "Please, my dear, have a seat."

Mila sat mutely.

The desk was clean with a leather writing pad and a laminate box holding business cards. The woman smiled broader. "Welcome to Hope for Children. My name is Francine. What can I help you with?"

Mila cleared her thoughts. "My name is Mila."

"Welcome, Mila."

Mila clamped her lips. *Odds were good Francine was pretty good with shy young women.*

"There lots of reasons people come here. To ask questions. To get an understanding. The journey to adoption takes many forms."

Mila nodded. *This wasn't Francine's first rodeo with a young woman.*

Francine's hands stretched on the desk, as if to say, we have no judgments here. "One doesn't have to be committed to adoption to come by and meet with us. Sometimes ladies just like to come check it out."

Mila gave her a small smile.

"It's fine. No matter what brings you here today."

"I really am just here for information purposes."

"Of course. Well, let me explain a bit about us. We have been in existence since 1962. In the beginning, our services were primarily for Christian couples. By the 1970s, as we began to help children overseas, we expanded our services beyond the faith. There were so many loving families in the United States that could open their homes to children."

"If someone wanted to adopt, how long does it take to get a kid?"

She smiled understandingly. "For adopting parents, the wait is anywhere from one to five years. Our waiting list is extremely long."

"Would those adopting parents pay for the child?"

"There is a great deal of work that goes into an adoption, either domestic or international. There is the screening of the children, the health care, the transit. We make sure that the families that are finally approved for adoption are stable both financially and in terms of their relationship. We are quite thorough in our screening. So, yes, there is a fee to cover those costs."

"I did a search. It said most US adoptions can cost up to $50,000."

"We are in that range, yes."

"It said international adoptions cost less."

"That can be true."

"Where do the children come from overseas?"

"Mostly Eastern Europe. Bulgaria. Ukraine, Romania."

"Because those countries are sending white kids."

Francine gave her a look. "We have children that come from all over."

Mila nodded. "Who can adopt?"

"Since 2014, we are open to all potential applications. But we preference couples."

"Gay couples?"

"They can apply, but they will likely not be top of the list."

"Why not?"

"We believe there are too many hurdles for the child to bear in today's society."

"Can a single woman adopt?"

"She can apply. But it's very unlikely. We preference traditional couples."

Mila crossed her arms over her chest. "That seems discriminatory."

"Yes, I can understand why you would say that."

"You can understand why I would say that, because it is discriminatory?"

Francine's smile did not falter. She was getting used to Mila's odd, abrupt manner.

"So, before 2014 you only gave to hetero married couples?"

"Correct."

"Only?"

"Correct."

That was a very interesting piece of information. How had single Aurélie Velk gotten a child? "So, the mother—the birth mother—doesn't get paid?"

Francine nodded. "Our general rule is to provide for medical services for young women that would like to put up a child for adoption. That provision can take you anywhere from the day you first find out you are pregnant, all the way through the nine months. We also pay for hospitalization and for specialized doctors if there's a problem with the birth."

"But you don't pay the birth mother?"

"No."

"So you get the child for free?"

Francine pulled a face. "That's not how we would phrase it, no."

"Are you a nonprofit?"

"No."

"So you make a profit?"

"That is certainly not why we are in existence. We are here to enable relationships to be formed between children who unfortunately do not have birth families. But, yes, we are a private adoption agency."

"If you don't pay the mom, it kinda sounds like you're selling humans."

Francine's eyes widened before she found composure. "No, my dear. That's not what you would be doing. Life is complicated. We are matching your child with loving parents."

"How do you find the kids?"

"We often work with orphanages. Particularly overseas. They identify children that are able to make the journey and that would do well in a home here."

Mila thought of Jimmy and her throat thickened. *He had been sold?* "How old can they be?"

"We work with all ages but infants the most."

"How do you know the child has actually been orphaned?"

"What do you mean?"

"How do you know he hasn't been stolen?"

"That's not how it works."

It might be. "Are you sure?"

"Yes. We do extensive due diligence."

"Like what?"

"Before we work with an orphanage, we make sure they are legitimate."

"But there is no way of knowing, for example, if an orphanage in Romania may, I don't know, be accepting kids who have been stolen."

"That's not how it works."

"Which part? That kids don't get stolen? Or that bad people don't accept stolen kids?"

Francine took a deep breath and ended that line of questions. "Mila, that's not how it works."

"Ok. And what happens, say, if the child wants to find the birth mother later? Like, later in life?"

"According to New York State law they must wait till they are eighteen years old. Then, in line with state law, they can come to us and request the identity of their birth mother. We are required to provide that information."

"Even if the kid comes from overseas?"

"Yes, that is correct." Francine stood. "Just a moment, let me get something." She walked through the door into a second room and returned with a thick photo album. She placed it on the desk and began flipping through the photos of smiling children. All of them were being held by white parents. "This is just a fraction of the children we have helped. Our purpose in life is to facilitate a lifetime of love. Your child will be placed with a loving, financially stable family."

Mila shrugged. "Sure."

"You can take your time making this decision. But if you are going to choose adoption for your unborn child, I would recommend that you start the wheels in motion sooner rather than later. We want to make sure you are getting proper medical care. That includes regular checkups and all the proper medications and vitamins that you should be having."

Mila pocketed one of the business cards, stood, and held out her hand. "Thanks for your time."

"Of course, Mila. It was lovely to meet you. You call me when you are ready."

Chapter Thirty-Eight

Dom jammed down on the gas pedal and the Tesla surged from the curb. She barely braked at the intersection, careening right in pursuit of the Porsche.

Diehl knew she was staking out Dartanian Velk.

Ahead, the residential street curved up the mountain, past gates and large houses. The Porsche was 500 yards ahead, moving at a reckless 50 mph.

A flash of yellow sailed around a bend. It was the yellow t-shirt of a teenage boy on a skateboard careening down the hill. He was barreling toward her right tire.

Dom twisted the wheel to the left and slammed the brake. The car squealed on a tight arc around the boy and brushed past him.

In her rearview mirror, the boy flashed the middle finger.

Up ahead, the road was empty.

She toed the gas and the car surged to 50 mph around the next curve.

A stop sign flew toward her, and she slammed to a stop.

Up ahead, the Porsche disappeared through a long curve to the right.

She hit the gas and the Tesla rocketed forward. The car hit 50 mph in a second and she hugged the curve in pursuit and flew through the curve.

The Porsche appeared far ahead up the hill.

Gates and houses were further and further apart as palm trees whipped past.

The Porsche disappeared around another curve.

She pressed the pedal and hit the new curve at 70 mph. The quiet of the engine at this speed was disconcerting. She rocketed out of the curve onto a long empty straight away. Above, the dusty brown of the empty canyon mountain stood out against a blue sky.

The Porsche had opened the space between them. He was a mile ahead on the empty road. He must have punched it out of the curve. He was doing nearly 90 or 100 mph.

Two can play that game.

Dom tapped the gas and the Tesla shot forward. The acceleration threw her head hard against the headrest. She loosened her grip.

Brown shrubs whipped past.

The speedometer hit 92 mph in a second.

In front, the Porsche was maintaining its distance, ripping through the curves of the empty road.

She pressed the gas. 95 mph. The Tesla was gaining on him.

She braked before another curve and pressed tight lines through the bend and exited at 102 mph.

Ahead, the Porsche had reached the summit and disappeared over the backside of the mountain.

"Shit."

Two minutes later, the Tesla crested over the mountain. Below, the empty road curved through wooded hills. The Porsche was hidden under a canopy of the trees.

She sped in pursuit. 105 mph.

The Tesla tore up the road as the minutes ticked by. 1. 2. 3.

Ahead, the road leveled out.

She slowed to 91 mph.

The Porsche was nowhere.

She slowed to 70 mph.

A sign read, *Getty Center Staff Parking.*

She braked hard to 25 mph.

The road gave way to gravel, and the tires skidded.

She was in an empty parking lot just above the traffic of the 405.

She slammed her palms on the wheel. "Dammit!"

The phone shrilled through the car.

Dom barked, "Answer."

"Dom, it's Lea and Owen. We've got something—"

Dom slammed her hands again and yelled, "Dammit!"

Lea said, "What?"

"They know I'm here."

Owen said, "What?"

"Diehl and Velk. They know I'm here."

Chapter Thirty-Nine

Mila nodded to the kind security guard in the rent-a-cop uniform and blinked as she stepped into the afternoon sun. The northbound traffic on 3rd Avenue was heavy across the four lanes.

The bike was still in its position, locked tightly against the pole of a *No Parking* sign. She slid her helmet on her head and her fingers pushed into the pocket of her jeans to grasp the Kryptonite key. As she leaned over to insert the key, something odd on the opposite side of 3rd Avenue caught her attention.

She paused as her eyes focused.

A hulk of a man was leaning against a storefront window. His arms were crossed over a thick chest.

She blinked.

Officer Robert Gessen's blue eyes bore into her.

Her blood ran cold.

Northbound cars flashed between them.

He slowly pushed off from the window.

Her fingers fumbled with the key.

In two long strides, Gessen reached the curb.

The key slid into the lock, and she turned it sideways. She grabbed the u-bar as it tumbled from the bike and jammed it in her bag.

Pausing at the curb, Gessen gave her an evil grin.

She slung the bag to her back.

Gessen glanced south, looking for a break in the stream of traffic.

Mila yanked the bike from the pole and drove the front tire off the curb.

Gessen darted to the corner and skidded to a stop at the pedestrian crossing.

Mila hurtled the bike between two parked cars, jammed her left foot down on the peddle, and swung her right foot over the back of the bike. Leaning over her handlebars, she drove down on her feet, lurching the pedals forward.

From among the crowd of waiting pedestrians, Gessen glared after her.

A city bus brushed past her right shoulder. A chemical cloud enveloped her.

Reaching the corner, she banked hard left onto 28th Street. She was heading west. The oncoming traffic was heading east.

Her fingers clamped on the brakes as the bumper of a yellow cab barreled down on her. Brakes squealed, tires screeched. The car shuddered to a stop six inches from her front tire.

The cab driver leaned out the window. "What the hell?"

Terrified, she yelled, "Sorry!"

She stood and leaned over the handlebars, pumping the pedals, keeping the bike close to the cars parked at the curb.

A white SUV whistled past.

Adrenaline surged through her veins, and she breathed in quick short bursts through her nose.

Was Gessen in pursuit? Had he hailed a cab to come after her?

At the corner of Lexington, she wrenched the bike southbound and pumped the pedals. She was barely keeping up with the fast-moving traffic.

She needed to lose him. She needed to cross the Lexington traffic and head west.

She would then jog the streets southward, using the alternating traffic patterns to her advantage. It would be impossible for a taxi to pursue her.

Glancing over her right shoulder, there was an opening between a Jeep and a Mercedes.

She pumped hard and merged into the space.

The Mercedes honked.

The next lane was streaming fast.

She let two cars pass her.

The Mercedes honked again.

To her right, a space opened, and she hurtled between cars.

But a sedan had simultaneously changed lanes and its front headlight tapped her back tire. The bike lurched forward from under her.

She leaned hard over the handlebars and pumped.

The sedan hit his brakes and space opened between them.

The bike shuddered and wobbled.

She shot her right hand out, warning the cars behind her.

A silver sedan slowed. A space opened up.

She jerked the bike into the far-right lane and cornered immediately to the curb on 27th.

She squeezed the brakes but the back brake failed.

The front tire rammed into the back of a parked Prius.

She flew forward and tumbled to the sidewalk. Outstretched palms slammed cement.

She rolled to her side. The skin on her hands burned.

A woman jogged to her. "Are you ok?"

Mila nodded and jumped up. "Yeah. Yeah. Thanks."

The woman breathed. "Oh, my god."

Her palms were on fire and had started to bleed. "I'm ok."

"Ok, wow. Be careful."

Mila turned to the bike. The back tire was dead flat.

She reached into her bag, grabbed her cell phone, and pulled up the map. There was a bike repair shop two blocks south. She could walk that in a few minutes.

Part V

*I shall overhear you, bare-foot,
scatting off into the darkness....*

—Lola Ridge, "Secrets"

Chapter Forty

KIEV, UKRAINE

Ludwig Hospital, whose official name was Kiev City Clinical Hospital #18, was a beautiful old 1800s building that had been badly retrofitted for the 1970s medical world. Stunning wood walls and marble floors looked bleak under cheap fluorescent lights. Utilitarian desks and cabinets lined grand rooms. Waiting benches hadn't been updated in decades.

Police Officer Ionna Moroz found the reception desk for the Obstetrics Department down a pink corridor at the back of the building. It was manned by a tired looking nurse in a wrinkled robe. "I'm looking for some information about children born at this hospital twenty-four years ago."

The nurse took in Ionna's uniform. "Let me call Zlata Kravets. Just wait here."

Ten minutes later, a very large woman in a printed dress and a long cardigan stomped down the hallway. "Ah, *Pani*. Please, come this way." She turned on a dime and waved a chubby hand.

Florescent tubes blinked over their silent journey along

corridors. Open doors displayed bleak patient rooms with four utilitarian wood beds with thin mattresses. Leaded windows let in weak sunlight. Somewhere an intercom called for a doctor named Nimchuk.

Zlata motioned her into a small, dark office where the light of a small lamp poured yellow across a scratched desk. Three of the four walls were lined with dented, metal filing cabinets.

Ionna sat.

Zlata wheezed, then smiled. "Ok, how can I help you, *Pani*?"

"I'm interested in running down a child that was born in this hospital during the 1990s."

Zlata nodded, her smile fading. "Ah, yes."

"Does that mean something to you?"

"Not in and of itself, but, yes, the time frame. I suspect I know why you are here."

"Then perhaps you can tell me. Because I have a hunch but I'm not exceptionally firm in my conclusion." She reached in her jacket pocket and withdrew her phone. "I believe this pendant may help us narrow the focus."

Zlata's eyes peered at the image. "Oh. I see."

Zlata was clearly adept at bureaucratic obfuscation. It was the plague of Kiev. "Does this mean something to you?"

"I'm not sure."

"Ms. Kravets. I am not here on official police business. Neither you nor this hospital will be in any trouble by what you tell me. It will remain confidential."

Zlata held her hands very still on the desk below an inscrutable face.

Ionna was not going to let this bureaucrat defeat her. It

was time to warm her up. "Ms. Kravets, I have been hired by a private client."

Zlata nodded.

"I am searching on behalf of this client into a mystery. My client is a lovely woman. An artist."

Zlata watched her.

"My client lost her sister recently. Killed. Shot. *Biznesmeni.*"

Everyone knew the mob. Everyone had been, at one point, impacted by the crime.

"My client's sister left behind a mystery. I would just like to solve it for the family."

Zlata's cold face slipped and her eyes turned sad. She nodded and said, "You've come to the right place."

"I'm glad to hear that."

"This building may not have all your answers, but it will have some."

Ionna encouraged her with a nod.

"It's a tragic story. Perhaps not one the sister, your client, wants to hear." Zlata glanced to the image. "The girls called these guardian angels. I don't know where they had them made. But they all ended up with them, before leaving the hospital." She leaned back in the chair, and it creaked under her weight. "They would bring them in only when they were in labor. Young girls. Sixteen, seventeen, eighteen. They had not been assigned doctors. They just were brought in when they were ready to give birth. We looked the other way. As we all did back then. The men that brought them in waited in the lobby or out in the parking lot. As if they were security. We knew…we knew they were elements." It was code for organized crime. "What could we do? Our staff has an obligation to treat the patient, not to ask the questions."

Ionna found herself holding her breath.

"The mothers would have the babies. We would bring the babies to them. The nurses, it was hard on them. These young mothers had only a few minutes with their newborns. Then they would turn to the nurses and say very clearly, 'Please give my baby to the man in the lobby from the orphanage.' Those words. Every time. Clearly instructed. But what could we do? So many things we had to do back then to ensure the safety of our staff…"

"And then what?"

"Well, we would swaddle the baby, collect formula and diapers in a bag, and give the baby to the designated man."

"Any chance he was the father?"

Zlata turned gruff. "No. Never. It was never a father. You could just tell. They never looked at the baby like it was their own. It was never the father."

"And then?"

"The young mother would be released a day or two later. If there were no complications."

"What was your conclusion?"

"International. I understand white children are preferred."

Ionna whispered, "Children stolen and monetized."

"Yes."

"Did anyone ever report them?"

"No." Her chin pushed toward Ionna. "You know what it was like back then. The police were part of it all. All part of the same."

"Did you keep records?"

Zlata said quietly, "As much as we could. We did not check the young mother's ID."

"But surely you would assign the patient a file, a number or something?"

Secrets of the Angels

"The mothers, they would give us names."

"Fake names."

"I'm sure." Zlata shook her head. "I'm sorry, *Pani*, but there is the dead end. Unless you know the fictitious name of your client's late sister, I don't know that this hospital can be of much help."

"I have a date."

Zlata's eyes widened. She whispered, "Give it to me."

"December 28, 1996."

Zlata heaved her bulk from the chair and moved around to a filing cabinet by the door. She slid open the second to lowest drawer, and chubby fingers riffled through tabs. Her fingers paused and she lifted a folder. She moved back to her desk, sat, and laid open the folder. "Let's see. 1996. December." Her head snapped up. "Yes, here. Here. A girl. Healthy. 9 lbs."

"What is the name?"

Zlata stood abruptly. She reached in her desk drawer and withdrew a wooden ruler like they used in primary school. She set it carefully horizontally across the page, under a specific line of text. Then she straightened and came around the desk, "You'll excuse me, *Pani*, I must use the lavatory. Just a few minutes. It will only take me five minutes." And she was gone out the door.

Ionna stepped around the desk and read, *Female. 9 lbs. Mother: Larysa Stefanyk.*

She blinked. A healthy 9 lbs. daughter had been born to a fake name and carried away. Never to be seen again.

A sadness moved around her like a heavy blanket, down over her shoulders. A single fake name in a logbook in a small office in a decrepit building was all that remained of a human being.

Five minutes later, Zlata lumbered into the office and sat

behind the desk. She noted Ionna's sadness. "I wish I had more for you. For your client. For the girl taken from her."

Ionna nodded.

"Well, at least you came. At least it led you here. That's something."

"Yes, I suppose you are right."

"Poor angels. Both the mother and the baby."

"Yes."

Ionna stood and handed her a card. "Zlata, please, keep my card. If you ever find more information, please, let me know. The family is a good family."

Zlata slid the drawer from the desk and slipped the card inside. "I am not hopeful."

"No, nor am I."

Chapter Forty-One

In the parking lot of the Getty Center above the 405, Dom stared at the California blue sky and castigated herself for falling for the Diehl chase. She was a Special Agent with the FBI with a long and successful track record of field operations, and she'd lost her cool. She'd hit the gas too soon. Literally.

She grimaced. Like an uncouth rookie, she'd blundered into their trap. Zero cunning.

The silence on the phone line stretched out.

She squeezed the steering wheel. They had dangled a worm in front of her position, and, like a Grouper, she'd mindlessly snapped for it. No thought, no focus.

She shook her head. They released a rabbit and, like an instinctive hound, she'd raced in pursuit. Rabid.

Now they knew for certain someone was following them.

She barked, "Dammit!"

Lea asked, "You ok?"

"No! It was a terrible move. It was all gut, all instinct. I jumped the gun. I should never have gone to his house. I should never have raced after Diehl. I've blown my cover. God dammit!"

Lea knew enough to keep quiet.

Owen didn't. "But what do they actually know?"

Lea jumped in. "Right? They know someone followed Diehl. They know someone is now outside Velk's. But maybe that's all they know."

Dom said, "But how did they know?"

"Maybe they saw you outside the Universal construction site."

Owen said, "We don't know what they know."

That was true.

Lea said, "The only thing this proves is that they know someone is on to them."

Dom slammed the wheel. "So fucking stupid. I'm so fucking stupid."

Owen said, "This is only just beginning. We need to regroup. That's all."

His words didn't register through her exasperation. "God dammit. I'm so fucking angry right now."

Lea whispered, "Oppression makes a wise man mad."

The statement pierced Dom's outrage and her brain paused. "The bible says that?"

"Oh, no. That's Frederick Douglass. 1852."

Owen said, "Dom, no operation is ever flawless. We've got him in our sights now. You need to regroup."

Dom swallowed. *He was right.* She needed to get her shit together. Blame wasn't going to fix the stumble. She pressed her head into the headrest and took a deep breath. "You're right. But how did they know?"

The traffic on the 405 was beginning to snarl.

Through the phone line, Lea groaned, "Oh, Lord."

Dom said, "What?"

Lea leaned close to the speakerphone. "Just a second, Dom."

The background noise sounded like chairs moving.

Lea returned to the speakerphone. "Dom, uh, Mila Pascale just walked in."

"What?"

Mila's voice was tight and small. "Hi, Dom."

Dom's fingers squeezed the wheel. "Mila? What are you doing there?"

Lea made introductions. "Mila, this is this Special Agent Owen Whyte."

Dom asked, "Mila?"

"I'm ok, Dom."

"What do you mean, you're ok? What the hell are you doing at the Bureau?"

Mila fumbled the words. "I'm ok. I'm—"

"Tell me what happened."

Mila declared, "I did research. I found out Velk had a sister. Never married."

Dom cracked her neck.

"Her name was Aurélie Velk. Years earlier, she adopted a baby girl. Aurélie's adopted daughter is named Lily Velk. She went to NYU."

Lea said, "Oh, Lord."

Mila said, "Dom, I'm sending you a photo of Lily."

Dom's phone vibrated in the passenger seat and she opened the photo. Lily Velk was a pretty, thin blond with a sad face.

Mila continued, "Aurélie Velk killed herself. Lily thinks her mom was haunted by the adoption."

Lea pushed. "Lordy, where is this going?"

Mila said, "I found the adoption agency. It's here. In New York."

Dom's jaw tightened.

"It's called Hope for Children. Over on the East Side. Kips Bay."

Lea said, "You better not have—"

Mila interjected. "I went there."

Lea gasped, "Lord help us."

Dom said, "Repeat that."

Mila said, "Like you said, Dom, I didn't look into Velk directly. I was not researching the case directly."

They were going to have another discussion about her interpretations of the ground rules. "Continue."

"What I found out is that there is no way Aurélie Velk adopted a child as a single woman back in the 1990s. There is almost zero probability she was able to do that. Legitimately."

Lea said, "Not legitimately? So illegitimately? As in illegally?"

"Yes."

Lea pushed. "That's a big leap, little miss. You think this Hope for Children sold her a kid?"

Mila concluded, "A) Aurélie Velk would not have qualified, back in the day, as a suitable candidate to adopt a child. B) Lily claims her mother was haunted by the adoption. C) Hope for Children was very insistent that they follow all due diligence. Overly insistent. I don't buy it."

Lea resisted. "That's a really big leap."

Mila said, "Yes."

Owen said quietly, "But an interesting one."

There was silence as all four minds chewed this new piece of information.

Below, on the 405, the traffic had slowed to a crawl.

Dom connected it first. "That's Dartanian Velk's original sin. His sister bought a kid. Illegally. He covered it up."

Owen jumped on the theory. "The mob found out. It would be ideal blackmail. Small enough to not get discovered but meaningful and personal enough to want to keep it hidden. That's how they first got their hooks in him. It's literally the ideal scenario for that initial blackmail."

Lea whistled.

Owen said, "They insisted they buy his first house off him. Now, in addition to covering up the human trafficking of his niece, he's into them for money laundering. Then they come to him later to get off one of their bent cops. Now he's into bribery of an official. That's the corruption of a public office. With each consecutive crime, they have more on him, he's in deeper. And because he's Internal Affairs, he knows exactly how compromised he is. He knows the consequences if they ever let on, any one of those crimes, let alone the whole enchilada."

Lea said, "His whole career. They've owned him this entire time."

Owen said, "Yeah, that's got to be it."

So simple. So clean. Of course, it was the answer. "Yes. It's gotta be it." Dom snapped back to the issue at hand. "Mila, why are you at Javits?"

Mila cleared her throat. "An hour ago, when I came out from the adoption agency, Gessen was there."

Shocked silence washed down the line like a massive wave.

Gessen. Dom growled, "I'm gonna tear his lungs out—"

Mila said, "He was going to follow me."

Dom snapped, "What happened?"

"I lost him. It's almost impossible to follow a bike through New York."

Lea choked. "Sweet baby lord, care for our innocent sheep."

Owen said, "Wait, how did he know Mila was there?"

Lea said, "Has Gessen been following Mila? How was he outside the adoption agency? He must have been following Mila. Or waiting for her to show up."

Mila said, "Yes. He was expecting me. He did not follow me on my bike. Impossible."

Dom slammed her palms. "God dammit!" *Everything about this operation has become a cluster fuck.*

Owen said, "Ok. Ok. Worst-case scenario is that Velk knows Mila has found the illegal adoption."

Lea said, "Maybe he thinks Dom is somehow related to Mila."

Mila asked, "Dom, does Gessen know who you are?"

"He doesn't know my name, no."

Lea asked, "When you went after Gessen, did you tell him you were Bureau?"

"No. He suspects I'm federal. He doesn't know which agency." She squeezed the wheel. "All he knows for sure is I'm Mila's guardian angel."

Owen said, "So they don't actually know what they're dealing with yet."

That was true.

Lea spat, "Uh, Dom?"

Dom stilled. "Yes?"

"I've got movement on one of Velk's phones."

Dom started. "Velk is on the move?"

"Yes."

Dom slammed the steering wheel again. "God dammit! Diehl. They had Diehl lure me away from the house! Where would he go?"

Owen said, "No reason he would change his normal daily routines. All they know is that someone was outside his house."

Dom hovered her foot over the gas pedal. "Where is he now?"

Lea rushed, "There's a delay on the phone's location. I need a minute. Where are you?"

Dom squeezed the steering wheel. "The god damned parking lot of the Getty Museum. Staring at the fucking 405. He doesn't get to just drive away from me."

Two minutes.

Nothing.

Four minutes.

Dom asked, "Lea?"

"Still a delay."

Only breathing across the open phone line.

Six minutes.

Seven minutes.

Lea cried, "Got him. He's near you! He's on the 405. Heading north."

Dom slammed her foot on the gas and yanked the wheel hard to the right. The car spun a wheelie, quiet as a ghost except for the gravel shooting from the tires.

She straightened the wheel and punched from the parking lot.

She raced down the Getty drive, screeched through an S-curve, and flew under the 405 overpass.

She cornered left and barreled up the on-ramp. "I'm about to hit 405 North."

Lea said, "Yes. He's still on the 405 heading north."

The far-right lane was moving slowly, and Dom had to brake to slide between cars.

She immediately merged to the left. She needed the fast lane, pronto.

Four more lane changes and she punched into a space.

The cars in the fast lane were doing a steady 70 mph. "Ok, talk to me. Where is he?"

Lea said, "Dom, remember we have a delay."

"Is he still on the 405 North?"

"Yes."

"Where does the 405 North lead?"

"It meets the 101, going north or south."

"He could be going anywhere."

"Agreed."

"How soon till he hits the 101?"

"Maybe ten minutes. How's the traffic?"

"It's ok."

Cutting through a canyon, brown bush rose on either side of the twelve-lane highway. Overhead a green interstate sign read, *405 North Sacramento, 101 North and South Ventura Los Angeles.*

Dom said, "I've got the split coming. North on the 405 or take the 101?"

The speed of the cars in the fast lane bumped up to 78 mph.

Dom said, "I've gotta make a decision soon."

Lea said, "Hold on, Dom."

Dom wafted up and over as the 405 N began a slight descent through the canyon. Ahead, she could see the split in the road and the green interstate signs.

She slowed and merged two lanes to the right, centering in the highway in case she needed to take the split to the 101. The traffic in the middle lane was cruising at 62 mph. It felt like molasses. Overhead, green signs spanned the width of the highway.

As the split approached, cars in the right lane began slowing.

The split was approaching quickly. 50 yards, 40 yards.

"Lea?"

"Hold on, Dom."

30 yards, 20 yards. "Lea?"

"He's still on 405 North!"

With one glance, Dom sized up an opening and swerved left into the middle lane, cutting off a blue Volvo. The Volvo's horn blared. Overhead the sign read, *405 North*.

Dom said, "I'm still on 405 North."

Lea said, "Yes. Stay there. He's ahead of you."

"How far out ahead?"

"With the delay it's hard to tell. I'm gonna say 10 miles."

"What's north on the 405? Where's he going?"

"It could be anywhere. Totally depends on how long he's gonna drive."

Dom slowed her breathing.

In Javits, Lea, Owen and Mila stayed silent.

Since they didn't know his exact location and they could only assume he was in the Land Rover, Dom had to stay a distance behind. She pushed the Tesla into the center lane and kept with the traffic. "I'm staying back."

Lea said, "That's all we can do, Dom. Stay steady. We have to see where he's headed."

Chapter Forty-Two

The traffic heading north on the 405 was maddeningly constant: drivers kept steady speeds. There was no need for weaving or lane changing.

Dom kept the Tesla moving at 65 mph in the middle lane. "He's still moving?"

Lea responded, "Yes, according to my screen, he's still on the move. Where are you?"

Dom read off the closest exit number. "What the hell is up the 405?"

Owen said, "We don't know."

In her rearview mirror, something blinked.

There. Again.

Roughly 200 yards behind on the highway, blinking red and blue lights were gaining on her. Quickly. "Shit."

Lea whispered, "What's happening?"

"LE," she said. Law enforcement. "Coming up on my rear."

Behind her, cars began moving right to get out of the fast lane.

There was an opening in the right lane. She merged between a Prius and a Dodge Charger and slowed to 55 mph.

Fifty yards out, two Ford Interceptor SUVs were barreling silently up the fast lane, lights blinking.

Owen's voice was hushed. "They coming for you?"

"I don't know."

Lea said, "Could Velk have called them in?"

Thirty yards behind, all traffic had moved from the fast lane.

Across all lanes, the traffic slowed. Nobody wanted to mess with two high-speed LAPD SUVs.

The SUVs gained ground.

Ten yards.

They were not slowing.

Blinking lights came parallel to her position. *What if they pull me over?* Adrenaline raced through her veins. She held her breath.

The two SUVs flew past.

She exhaled. "They just passed me."

Mila spoke softly. "What are the odds that the LAPD Head of IA is gunning north from an FBI agent and two LAPD cruisers just happen to race past?"

Dom said, "None."

Lea said, "Exactly."

Owen said, "He's called in backup."

Dom said, "For what?"

Mila said, "What if he's trying to escape?"

Dom clenched her jaw. *After getting this close, he doesn't get to just walk away. Even with his thugs.* She merged left into the farthest lane and punched the gas. "Ok, I'm keeping eyes on."

She kept the Tesla ten yards behind the blinking SUVs

racing north.

Mila said, "Van Nuys private airport."

Lea said, "What?"

Dom rasped, "What? What did Mila just say?"

Mila responded, "I looked it up on my phone. It's Van Nuys airport. It's private. Ahead of you on the 405."

Lea spat. "I'll be fucking good god damn. He's headed to an airport."

What if he left the country? "Could he be leaving the country?"

Owen said, "I don't know. I really don't know."

Lea interrupted, "Mila's right. The ping is near the airport!"

Ahead, the SUVs merged right. They were going to exit.

Mila said, "Dom, you're looking for exit 66B toward Sherman Way."

Lea yelled, "Yes! He's pinging at Van Nuys now."

Dom careened the Tesla right. "Lea, get to Fontaine and brief him. He needs to know up to the minute. I have no idea why Velk is at an airport, but it is not looking good."

Lea must have taken off on a run, because Mila whispered, "I'm watching Lea's screen. He's pinging at the airport."

The blinking SUVs exited under a sign for *Sherman Way*.

Behind them, Dom raced down the ramp. "I'm exiting."

Mila said, "Left under the highway."

Dom cornered left onto a street that was empty. "They're not here."

Mila said, "Right onto Haskell."

Dom cornered right. Five blocks ahead, the taillights of the second SUV blinked as it disappeared around a left corner.

Mila said, "You're going to take a left in five blocks."

"Yes, I see them." Dom slowed and stopped at each stop sign.

Owen said the obvious out loud. "Velk has called up LAPD backup. For protection."

"Crap on a stick…"

Owen said, "Yes, he's expecting you."

Dom said, "Well, good on fucking him. Cause I'm coming in hot."

Chapter Forty-Three

The SUVs rolled into a parking lot of a modern, curved steel and glass building and pulled to the entrance. The blinking lights turned off. Behind the terminal, two black runways glared in the sun. Domed plane garages dotted the landscape. A wire fence circled as far as Dom could see.

She slowed past the parking lot, carried on down the street, then U-turned. Returning, she rolled under the shade of a tall palm tree and parked at the curb 20 yards away.

In front of the terminal, four uniformed LAPD exited the two SUVs. Two disappeared through the glass sliding doors. The remaining two stood watch, thumbs hooked into fully loaded belts, looking out over the parking lot from behind mirrored Ray-Bans.

A Range Rover was parked among other high-end cars.
I'm here, Velk.

The air was dry and gritty. At the farthest end of the runway, a small plane took off with a distant roar. Its wings wobbled slightly as it soared against the blue sky.

Lea's voice boomed through the car's speaker. "Dom,

I'm back. Fontaine's on his way across the floor. He is not fucking happy."

Fontaine yelled as he approached, his voice getting louder with each step. "Walker! What in the hell is going on?"

She gave him a beat to reach Lea's desk. "Sir, I'm at Van Nuys."

"I know that part. Peck brought me up to speed. Sitrep now." He wanted a situation report.

"Two LAPD units arrived ahead of me, lights flashing. My guess, he's pumped them a story that he needs protection."

"Where do you think he's going?"

She said, "I'm not sure."

Owen interrupted, "Sir, I'm Special Agent Owen Whyte—"

"I know who you are, son."

Owen continued, "A number of countries don't have extradition treaties. A few in the middle east, some in Africa, Asia, some Eastern Europe."

Fontaine asked incredulously, "Do we think he's scared enough to flee the country?"

Dom said, "We don't know. We don't know how much he knows. He probably knows I'm federal. Maybe he suspects Bureau."

Fontaine barked, "Peck, get me today's flight schedules out of Van Nuys and their destinations. Now!" His voice boomed through the car as he leaned into the speakerphone. "Walker, just what in the fuck are you doing chasing him to the airport?"

Silence.

He growled, "I asked you a question, Special Agent."

I want eyes on him. "This is still in play."

Fontaine erupted. "God dammit, this is not an op!"

Lea interrupted. "Sir, I have Van Nuys on the phone. They are not providing that information."

"Give me that phone." There was a pause before Fontaine yelled, "This is Assistant Director in Charge of the New York FBI Field Office. With whom am I speaking?" Another short pause. "You will pull up those schedules and read them out to SOS Peck or I will have your job." A minute later, he barked, "Who the hell is this?"

He must have noticed Mila.

Lea jumped in. "She's with me. She's an intern."

"Jesus Christ. Walker, give me the rest."

"Velk is inside. His vehicle is here. Two LAPD inside. Two LAPD outside. Meatheads."

"Where are you?"

Through the nearby fence, three jets stood at the ready on the tarmac. One had pilots in the cockpit and stairs rolled to an open door. "Outside the airport on the street alongside the runway. In the shade."

"They have eyes on you?"

"No."

Lea said, "Velk isn't on a passenger manifest. He probably isn't using his real name. But the flights leaving within the next three hours are: Houston, Cleveland, Pittsburgh, New York, Miami, and Boston."

Dom asked, "Then what?"

Owen added, "If he's headed overseas, the check-in desk at most airports have to confirm passengers have their passports. But I'm not sure we'll have enough time to screen all those airports in advance to pull him from the flight before departure."

Fontaine spoke softly. "First of all, we don't know he's on

the run. Second, we don't know if he's leaving the country. Third, we don't have enough to pull him from a flight, even if we wanted to. And fourth, this is not a fucking operation."

He doesn't just get to fly away. "But, sir—"

"No. Your orders, Walker, are to sit tight."

A flight attendant in a tight-fitting blue uniform exited the terminal and strode toward the open jet pulling two roller luggage bags.

Dom asked, "Can we ground a plane?"

Fontaine said, "No, we are nowhere near any kind of official action."

"So, we just let him fly out now?"

"For now, if that's what he's doing, yes. There are enough jurisdictional entanglements with this as it is. You are not to approach."

She clamped her lips.

He snarled, "Walker, did you hear me?"

The flight attendant hefted her roller bags and climbed the ten steps.

She responded, "Sir, he just gets to fly away?"

In the cockpit, the two pilots turned in their seats to welcome the flight attendant.

Fontaine said, "As of this moment, that is our only option. Yes."

Dom lifted her phone, snapped a photo of the readying plane, and texted it to Lea.

In the background, Lea said softly, "Got it."

Dom rummaged in her bag and pulled a single wireless earbud. She pressed it into her ear, slid her Glock from under the seat, and locked it into her shoulder holster. She pushed open the car door and stood. Above her, palm fronds rustled.

Fontaine asked, "Walker, why does it sound like you've just gotten out of the car?"

From outside the terminal lobby door, LAPD mirrored glasses caught her movement and locked on.

In her ear, Fontaine asked, "Walker, are you out of your car?"

She ignored the mirrored meatheads and stepped from the curb.

Fontaine asked, "Walker, what in the fuck are you doing?"

Inside the cockpit, one of the pilots noticed her.

From the side of the terminal, two airport staff in coveralls approached the prepping plane.

Gravel crunched under her feet as she crossed the street.

The breeze rustled the phone line.

"Agent, I asked you a specific question. What are you doing?"

Sending him a message. "I'm taking a walk."

Fontaine bellowed, "What?"

The sunglasses outside the lobby followed her movements as she stepped across the dry grass alongside the fence. "You said I was not to approach. I'm not approaching."

He asked, "Then what the fuck are you doing?"

Reaching the fence, she planted her feet and crossed her arms. "I'm sending a message."

Chapter Forty-Four

A dry breeze off the runway rippled the grass at her feet. Behind the glimmer of the cockpit window, the heads of the two pilots bobbed and weaved as they readied for flight. An intense, high-pitched whine rumbled from the airplane as the engine spun to life.

At the rear of the terminal, a glass door slid open and Dartanian Velk stepped into the sun. He wore a dark suit, white shirt, and dark sunglasses. His black hair was swept back and glinted with pomade. A soft leather briefcase in his left hand tapped his thigh as he strode across the tarmac toward the revving plane.

There will be justice for my father. Dom said, "I've got eyes on. He's heading to a plane."

Silence.

Velk strode across the tarmac ten feet before he noticed her.

Midstride, he paused. His foot hung for a moment in the air.

The pitched whine from the engine filled the space between them.

She held her breath.

In her ear, Fontaine said, "Agent, talk to me."

Velk pivoted toward her and planted his foot. He stood for a long moment, taking in her presence.

Dom said, "He sees me."

Velk leaned forward imperceptibly.

Behind her sunglasses, she narrowed her eyes.

Velk took a single step toward the fence, but hesitated, weighing the benefits of a confrontation.

You are a coward. You have always been a coward.

He took another step, but paused.

She waited, arms at her side. Nonthreatening.

In an instant, he was walking toward her.

Dom whispered, "He's coming to me."

In her ear, Fontaine spoke slowly and with gravity. "Leave this line open. We will tape you. Slow your breathing. Take a mental step back. Right now, you are a highly trained and specialized FBI Special Agent. Your only goal is to walk the perp into a confession."

Raising her hand, under the guise of taking off her sunglasses, Dom also pinched the ear bud between two fingers. "Copy."

Velk was moving determinedly.

Blinking against the searing sun, she lowered her hand and let it rest slightly behind her hip. *Fidelity. Bravery. Integrity.*

Velk stopped five feet from the fence. He slipped off his sunglasses. His dark eyes were hard.

For a long moment, they sized each other.

Get him talking. She waited.

His shoulders were back, ready for conflict. "Who are you?"

She said indifferently, "That's not the most important thing right now."

"You Fed?"

She shrugged.

"Are you the one following me?"

She nodded.

"Is this all about that Mila Pascale?"

Let him talk. She shrugged again.

"She should have kept her nose out of other people's business."

She dipped her chin. "That's probably true."

"Young girl, getting into trouble. Creating trouble for all of us."

She nodded.

"Well, she's been sent a message today to back off."

He meant Gessen. Dom's blood turned to icy sludge. She kept her voice calm. "Yes. I know."

"Then you and she should back off now."

He only knows she's with Mila. She shrugged.

"What's your relation to the girl?"

She said, "We are not related."

"Were you the one to approach Officer Gessen?"

"What did he tell you?"

"That a woman staked out his house. At night."

She said, "He didn't like getting staked out."

Velk shook his head. "He didn't."

"Or approached in the middle of the night. In a threatening manner."

Velk kept his mouth shut.

She gave him a sly smile. "Shoe on the other foot. But your thug, Gessen, played it too heavy-handed. Midnight outing to scare Miss Pascale into silence. I mean, wow, way to go, champ. Way to get me thinking. I mean, there must be a lot to cover up if an NYPD blue is gonna go chasing an innocent child in the night."

Velk waited.

"Seems if one young woman with absolutely no background hit a sore spot pretty easily. It got me thinking, maybe there's something there?"

He set down his briefcase.

The roar of the plane vibrated her chest. "I mean, I've got time on my hands. And as far as you know, I have some heavy artillery behind me. I mean, what if *I* found something..." She gazed over his head, into the blue sky, as if she had all the world to wait. *Let him sweat.*

He crossed his arms.

"Like, what if I found that the Head of Internal Affairs for NYPD and now LAPD was involved in whatever shitty business Gessen was into? Wouldn't that be interesting? Dartanian Velk, what an interesting story you have."

He held out one palm. "We thought there had been an understanding after you talked to Gessen."

"How so?"

"We leave her alone. She stops doing...whatever it is she's doing."

"And?"

He closed his hand into a fist. "It appears she's still meddling."

"Your thug overplayed again. You really should teach him about subtlety." She cocked her head. "Good ole Gessen was waiting for Miss Pascale at a specific building. A building in Kips Bay of all places." They were treading on the adoption agency territory. How badly was he willing to keep that hidden? *Tighten the screws.* "What if I'd found out some interesting facts on Dartanian Velk?"

He took a decisive step toward her.

Secrets of the Angels

The Glock in her holster warmed at his nearness.

See if he breaks. She leaned toward him, "What's in that building, Velk? What are you so desperate to hide that you sent Gessen to watch over it? What will I find if I go looking through all the tenants in that building?"

He said, "Let's make a deal."

Breaking point. She smiled. "I'm listening."

"It would be very easy for both sides to walk away from this. Right now. We leave Mila Pascale alone, you leave me alone."

She shrugged.

"Are you expecting more to the offer?"

He was going to offer her money to leave him alone. She shrugged.

He took the bait. "How much?"

Dartanian Velk was willing to pay someone to leave him alone. It was an admission of guilt. She waited.

He asked, "How much?"

Lure him in. "A big amount."

"How many zeros?"

"At least six."

"I can get it wired to you within the hour."

The Head of the LAPD's Internal Affairs was so dirty he had access to a million dollars within an hour. And the FBI in New York had it on tape. It was enough to get him fired and likely jailed.

Dom stepped to the fence. "I'm not here for your dirty money."

"What are you here for?"

"Justice for my father."

Confusion swept Velk's face. He opened his mouth, but nothing came out.

"I've been chasing you, Velk."

He blinked.

"My name is Domini Walker."

Velk stepped back from the fence. His mouth gaped open as recognition trickled in.

"I'm Stewart Walker's daughter. You remember Stewart."

His eyes widened as realization hit him. "Stewart..."

She hissed. "Cat got your tongue?"

He shook his head, trying to clear a memory. "He...it wasn't supposed to turn out that way."

"How was it supposed to turn out?"

His eyes were wild. "It was a mistake."

"Which part was a mistake, Velk?"

He blinked rapidly. "His death."

Her blood roiled. She snarled, "You came to our home. You sat with him. I was there. I was a kid. You came to our home."

He shook his head defensively. "I told him, these cases you're looking into, these cops that got off, you need to leave that alone."

"You didn't want him looking into those cases."

He was trying to clear himself. "I told him. At first, he said he would leave it alone. But he didn't. He kept digging. He was getting too close."

"What was it about those cases? Why wasn't Stewart Walker supposed to find out why you cleared those cops?"

He clamped his lips shut.

"Too close to what?"

Velk was trembling. "I...I..."

"Tell me what you told him."

He stammered, "We worked out a sting. He would pretend to be part of the crime. We'd catch the dirty cops. Later I would get him out of jail."

"That's what you told Stewart. You sent him into that apartment building, thinking he was undercover, that he was the good guy. You let him think he was working on behalf of the IA."

Velk nodded.

"Did you tell him you'd exonerate him after?"

His voice was quiet. "Yes."

"But that wasn't really the plan, was it? You were setting *him* up. You, Gessen, the other dirty cops, you were setting Stewart up. The actual plan was to set up my father."

Velk's eyes widened and he blinked against the memories.

She snarled. "You set him up. That was the real plan. You never intended to clear him. You were never going to swoop in and exonerate Stewart Walker. The real plan was that my father would get indicted. At trial, Gessen and his goons would turn on my father. Because you wanted him stripped from the force. You needed him shut down."

He whispered, "Yes."

She yelled, "Say it!"

He slumped. "I set him up."

There it was. The truth. And it was on tape. She expelled the air from her lungs. *Her father was innocent.*

As if the conversation was complete, Velk leaned down to pick up his briefcase.

Dom stepped to the fence. "What had my father discovered about you, Gessen, the others, that was so profound?"

Velk shook his head to fend her off. There was fear in his eyes.

She pressed. "What had Stewart discovered?"

Velk turned, walked toward the plane.

She yelled, "I know a lot more than you think."

He paused.

She shouted, "I know about your sister!"

He turned and walked slowly back to the fence.

Dom said, "I know she illegally adopted Lily. I know it haunted her. I know she took her own life."

He closed his eyes, momentarily blocking out his pain.

"Somebody else found out about it, too, didn't they? They found out about how your sister adopted Lily. Your weak spot, your Achilles. The same people that have been paying too much for your houses."

His eyes popped open.

"They've been squeezing you for years now, haven't they? Oh, I'm pretty sure I know who has their talons into you, too. You sent my father to jail to cover all the dirty shit you and the others are involved in."

He stumbled backwards.

She stepped to the fence, pointed a finger at his face. "My father didn't commit suicide, did he?"

He blinked.

She repeated it in a hiss. "My father didn't commit suicide, did he?"

Velk's head moved a fraction, an infinitesimal shake.

"Say it. Say Stewart Walker didn't commit suicide."

He shook his head.

She slammed her palm against the fence. The metal rattled loudly. "Say it!"

"Stewart didn't kill himself."

She blinked. The blood rushed from her veins.

In her head, Stewart sighed, *"There you go, my smart, strong Dom. There you go."*

She yelled, "Who killed him?"

He shook his head. "Domini—"

"Don't say my name. You don't deserve to say my name. Who killed my father?"

"You can't bring this down. It's bigger than you know."

"Tell me."

"You can't stop them."

She pulled her badge and jammed it against the fence. "We can take a shot. I like our odds."

He stumbled back. "You're FBI?"

Fidelity. Bravery. Integrity.

He turned and bolted to the waiting jet.

Dom pushed the ear bud into her ear and spoke clearly. "He's gone."

Fontaine said, "We got it. We got it all. It's over, Dom. Your part is over. Well done. Really, well done."

Part VI

I shall know you, secrets
by the litter you have left
and by your bloody foot-prints.

—Lola Ridge, "Secrets"

Chapter Forty-Five

KIEV, UKRAINE

Ionna opened the door to Nadiya Omelchenko with a sad face.

Nadiya said, "Oh my. That doesn't look good, *Pani*."

Ionna said, "I'll make some tea. Have a seat."

When she returned, Nadiya's bag was on the couch and the woman had climbed through the window onto the balcony.

Ionna set the tea on the window ledge and climbed through the window.

Nadiya was watching two boys passing a soccer ball in the park. She had found the pack of cigarettes. "May I?"

"Of course." Ionna sat on the window ledge.

Nadiya lit a cigarette with a shaky hand. "How bad is it?"

"Well, it depends on how you look at it. You told me when we first met that your sister, Aneta, had a decent husband. And that he treated her ok."

Nadiya's eyes watched the boys as she blew smoke through tight lips. "Yes, that's true."

"And it sounds like they had enough money to live a decent life."

"More than enough. Yes, that's true."

"And here in the Ukraine, that is more than most."

Nadiya nodded, but her eyes remained on the park.

"But, I'm afraid, your sister had secrets."

Nadiya swallowed then inhaled.

"She told you she was a model. Overseas. But I'm afraid that isn't the truth."

Nadiya's eyes blinked slowly as her brain imagined what was to come. In the Ukraine, it was easy to imagine the worst.

"She was here. In Kiev. Caught up in a business that many women who are pretty fall into."

Nadiya held one elbow against her waist, the one arm up, the cigarette stilled in front her lips. She stared blankly across the tops of the park trees.

"Your sister was involved with a brothel. She worked there."

A tear dropped down Nadiya's cheeks.

Ionna shrugged to herself. What more was there to say about that side of things?

Nadiya's jaw tightened. "Did Greigor find her there?"

"I don't know. I truly don't know."

Nadiya spat over the edge of the balcony. She turned to Ionna. "And the box of secrets?"

Ionna blew out her cheeks. "She had another secret. She delivered a child. On December 28, 1996. Here in the city. Clinical Hospital #18."

Nadiya trembled. She handed the remaining burning butt to Ionna as she leaned over on her knees and hyperventilated.

Ionna crushed out the butt. She could say she was sorry,

for the secrets she unleashed, but in the Ukraine, you don't apologize for what is the truth.

Nadiya's breathing subsided and she rose. "The box. The mementos. They were for the child?"

Ionna nodded.

"A boy or a girl?"

"A girl. Healthy."

"And the girl now?"

"She is gone. We will never know. Your sister didn't know where."

Nadiya's lips trembled. "They stole the baby?"

Ionna nodded.

Nadiya clamped her lips. She blinked rapidly as she took in the new information. "They stole…"

Ionna nodded.

Her brow furrowed. "Do you think there is a way…?"

"No. It was very systematic. The mothers would come, they would not give real names, give birth, men would come and take the babies away. It was a process. A strict process."

Nadiya turned and looked out over the park for a long moment. "So, no need to tell my parents. Aneta was an angel in this life. She is an angel still. I will let her keep her secrets." She turned to leave. "Thank you, *Pani*."

Later, after Ionna had smoked two cigarettes while watching the children in the park, she discovered a single gold bar on her living room table.

Chapter Forty-Six

Lea had honked for Dom at the curb of the arrivals exit at LaGuardia. Owen and Mila beamed from the backseat. They'd found a local diner and crammed into a booth.

Across the table, Lea held up her coffee mug in a toast. "To closing the mystery."

Next to Lea, Mila held up hers. "To closing the mystery."

Owen's arm brushed Dom's as he held up his.

The four clinked mugs and took a hit of caffeine.

Lea looked to Dom. "How you feeling?"

Dom sighed. "You know, I slept all the way on the plane."

"You did?"

"Totally."

Mila said, "That's mental exhaustion."

Owen nodded.

Dom said, "Yeah, I guess. I sat down, and I was out like a light."

Lea pointed at her. "It was that extra leg room I got you!"

They all smiled. The relief was overwhelming.

Mila asked, "You call Beecher?"

Dom nodded. "Yeah. I gave him the low-down before I boarded. We'll talk when I get home later. But, yes, he knows."

Mila asked, "He knows your dad didn't kill himself?"

What a funny awkward woman. Who knew so unique could be so charming? Dom smiled, "Yes, he knows that part."

Mila nodded matter-of-factly. "Good."

Lea asked, "Fontaine?"

"I'm seeing him later."

"You talk to him yet?"

Dom shook her head. "No, not yet. I can't decide if I'm looking forward to it or not."

Lea nodded vigorously. "Amen."

Owen said, "You want us to go with you?"

"No, I think I'm ok for this first meeting."

Lea nodded. "Ok. And, uh, Velk's still in Boston." They were able to trace Velk's flight from the airplane's tail number in the photo Dom had sent.

Dom asked, "Do we know what he's doing there?"

"It sounds like normal business. We don't know the details. But we have agents on him now. They're moving quickly. They've already asked Owen and myself for our evidence."

Dom said, "Good."

Owen said, "It's a pretty compelling, but sensitive case. We scratched the surface. They'll go deep. It may take a bit."

Lea mumbled, "Understatement."

Owen nodded. "Agreed. It's a pretty explosive case."

Dom asked, "But they'll keep eyes on him?"

Lea said, "Oh yea. Since it's OC, I talked to Fumble and Drop—"

Next to her, Owen cleared his throat.

Lea never took her eyes off Dom, but she grinned. "They said, once there's a link, the Bureau keeps pretty good tabs."

Was there something going on between these two or was her tired brain playing tricks? "What else did Fumble and Drop say?"

Owen stiffened.

What is going on?

Lea grinned wider. "Those Brighton Beach crowds are their specialty. Fumble and Drop I mean."

Owen cleared his throat again.

Ok, something was going on.

Lea's grin was ear to ear. "They said the Bureau tends to build a case from the bottom up. They try to get the most people involved in one net. Smaller guy squeals on larger fish. RICO, whatnot. You know the story. I asked 'em what happens when you land a big fish on the first try—" She raised her mug and they all clinked again. "They said it was super unusual. But they don't know our Warrior Princess Dom, do they?"

Owen smiled widely.

Lea glanced at him with a knowing grin.

There. Something was definitely going on here.

Mila was oblivious to the undercurrents at the table.

Lea continued. "So when I asked them what happens when you land a big kahuna on the first go, they said they didn't actually know, but they imagined the investigation would proceed similarly. They started talking about feelers, wire taps, surveillance, plea deals, and of course, financial surgeries."

Dom turned to Owen. *God, those eyes were blue in the morning sun.* "That sound right to you?"

He said, "Yes. And I've asked Fontaine if I can be on that case."

"Really?" A flush crawled up her neck.

"Yes."

"What did he say?"

"He said he'd think about it. When you go in there, can you mention it?"

Dom said, "Uh, sure."

"We want the best on this one, right?"

Lea chuckled. "So cocky."

His head bobbed. "Yes. But I'm right, aren't I?"

Lea conceded. "Yes."

Dom smiled at his bravado. "I agree. We want the best on it."

Lea winked at her. "Right? Don't we want the best?"

Oh my god, Lea had talked to Owen about Dom. Lea was clearly encouraging him to pursue Dom. Dom threw the traitor a glare.

Lea smiled in return, one eyebrow raised. "I mean, we want the best, don't we?"

Owen grinned at Dom.

Dom stumbled through the innuendos flying across the table. "Did Fumble and Drop have any idea how long it would take until we have indictments?"

Lea shook her head. "It all depends on the case. But, let's remember that the patient in spirit is better than the proud in spirit. Ecclesiastes."

Owen crooked his head. "What?"

Lea shrugged. "It's a thing I do."

"It's one of *many* things our friend, Lea, here, does."

Dom gave her a stink eye. "Did Fumble and Drop know which crew it was out in Brighton Beach?"

Lea shook her head. "That will be part of the case. They need to circle in, figure out who Velk's contact is. Then build up to who actually owns him."

Mila set her mug down. "I have an idea."

Three sets of eyes turned to her.

Lea said, "Go ahead."

"Those photos I sent you? From the cemetery?"

"Yes?"

"One of them is a wide angle of the funeral crowd. I noticed that there is a big tree in the background. Pretty far from the crowd. There are some men standing underneath. Dark coats. Even dark hats. I mean, if you're trying to connect to mob...these guys look fit for purpose. The photographer in Philly, he'll have more photos. We could get a good ID off them, I'd imagine."

Lea snorted.

Owen said, "Mila Pascale, you are a genius."

Mila shrugged nonchalantly. "I know."

Chapter Forty-Seven

Fontaine looked up from a pile of documents on his desk with tired eyes. "Welcome back, Agent."

Through the window behind him, the afternoon sun was bright.

Dom leaned against the wall by the door. "Sir."

He said, "Well done."

"Thank you."

"I should be mad."

She nodded, "Yes, sir."

"But, I'm not."

"I'm grateful for that."

"I understand family."

She thought of Beecher and her father. "I would do anything for family."

"Agreed. So, let's talk next steps. I've opened an official investigation. The evidence already produced by your motley team is definitely enough—"

She said, "We may have some more."

"That's fine. You give it to me, I'll pass it over to the new team. I want a Chinese wall around you. Do you hear me? I do not want you anywhere near this." He rolled his eyes. "Oh, how many times have I said that to you?"

She hung her head.

"But the thing is, I trust you to keep away from this. It's far too important for you to get messed up in this and create a reason for an appeal."

He was absolutely right. "Yes, agreed."

"So, for once, Special Agent Walker, you have incentive, not just me telling you, to stay away."

She nodded.

"Ok, so get me whatever your team has and close your team down."

She said, "Uh…"

"Yes?"

"Owen Whyte would like to be on the case."

"No. He's too close."

"Sir, he's not."

Fontaine watched her. "Are you sure?"

What was he implying? "Sir?"

"That's two unofficial cases you two have worked together now. And need I remind you that you saved his life? I think he is too personally involved."

She swallowed. "But he's one of the best."

"We have other forensic accountants."

"But he's one of the best."

He leaned back in his chair, steepled two fingers below his chin, and squinted at her. "It keeps you in the loop."

She pinched her brows. "But does it really? I wouldn't say, 'in the loop.'"

"Fair point. But if Owen stays on the case, he can feed you news."

She looked away and shrugged, as if the thought hadn't occurred to her.

"On the other hand, your commitment to this case may let you see things the official team doesn't."

Was he throwing her a bone? "Exactly."

"Ok. For now, I'll get him assigned in a support capacity. He can't lead on forensics."

"Thank you, sir."

He said, "But Lea Peck is off this. 100% off this. You are off this. 1,000% off this."

"Of course."

"We'll get you a new assignment."

She pushed off from the wall.

"Agent, remember that this will take months."

She nodded.

"It will feel like forever. But know that we are on it. The Bureau is nothing if not thorough."

She said, "Understood."

"We will nail Velk. He will pay for what he's done."

Chapter Forty-Eight

Lily Velk's long blond hair lay smoothly against her face as she read the New York Times paper version. The evening light tinted the lighter strands a very pale pink.

Mila took her coffee and walked slowly down the aisle of the coffee shop.

Lily was absorbed in the news.

Mila stopped, and stood facing the table awkwardly.

Eventually Lily looked up with green eyes and a funny smile.

Mila said, "You're Lily Velk."

Lily smiled. "I am."

"My name is Mila Pascale."

Lily grinned. "Hi, Mila."

"I'm a student at NYU." *Not a lie.*

"Oh, hi." Lily casually waited for the explanation.

"I saw a video from one of your psych classes."

"Ok? You a psych student?"

Mila said, "No." *Also not a lie.*

"Oh." Lily made a small, curious laugh. "What can I do for you, Mila?"

Mila pulled out the opposite chair, sat, and placed her coffee down gently. "I've lost someone."

"I'm sorry?" Confusion returned to Lily's face.

Mila swallowed. "My younger brother. He was taken."

Empathetic pain swept her face. "Oh, no. That's terrible. I'm sorry."

"Thanks. Well, see, that makes me have a particular perspective."

"On what?"

"I would do anything to find him again."

Lily frowned. "I'm sure you would. What a terrible, terrible thing."

"I think you could consider me a unique messenger."

"Ok?"

Mila reached in her pocket and slid the Hope for Children card across the table. "I know you know about them."

Lily stared at the card.

"In that psych class video, you mentioned your adoption, and how you were processing the feelings."

Lily blinked up at her. "Mila, this is a bit weird."

Mila held up her hands. "I know, I know. I won't take long, then I'll be gone. So, I was curious about what you said, and I actually read your term paper."

Lily leaned back and crossed her arms over her chest.

"And you referenced them." Mila pointed to the card. "Did you know that New York State Law states that if you're adopted and over eighteen you can request your birth information?"

Lily's mouth tightened.

"Ah, you know that already."

Lily said, "Yes."

"But you haven't done it."

Lily shook her head. Confusion swept her face.

"Because you want to remember your adopted mother as your mother."

Lily's voice was whisper soft. "Yes."

Mila nodded. "I absolutely understand that." She pushed the card across the table. "But consider my unique perspective for a moment. I would give anything to know that my younger brother is ok. That now, he is ok. I would give anything."

Lily's face fell.

Mila stood. "You should find out who your birth mother is. Because someone out there wants to know that you are ok, that you are safe, that you are happy. They just want to know that."

Chapter Forty-Nine

Stopping by Lea's desk on her way home, Dom looked over the young SOS's shoulder and scanned the screen. Just as she suspected, Lea was reviewing more court transcripts. She said, "Fontaine's instructed us to step away."

"He may have said that to you, but he didn't say it to me."

"Oh, no. He said you in particular, too. Those were his exact instructions."

Lea glanced up at her. "If I haven't heard it yet, I don't know about it yet. I've got a few more hours."

Dom shook her head. "You finding anything?"

Lea tightened her jaw dramatically. "I'm hating what they did to John Karem. I'm hating that they got to him. I want to know who set him up."

"You think that's gonna be in those files?"

"I dunno, but it's worth a try. Before I get Fontaine's email and I turn into a fucking pumpkin on this case."

"I hear you. You do have to sleep at some stage."

Lea sighed, "Yeah, I know. You headed home?"

Dom squeezed her face. "Uh, sure."

Lea cocked her head. "That's not exactly a yes."

"Uh-huh."

Lea eyed her suspiciously. "Wait. What're you doing?"

Across the hall, the elevator door opened and Owen stepped out. He was carrying a motorcycle helmet in each hand.

Lea's mouth opened. "Wait. What? What's going on?"

Dom said, "I've got something I have to wrap up."

Lea grinned widely. "Wait! Are you two finally going on a date—"

"No. No. It's not about Owen…"

"What then?"

"The less you know, the better."

"Oy!"

Dom said, "Trust me."

Chapter Fifty

It was dark when the Triumph cornered onto the dark Staten Island street and slowed. Dom unclasped her hand from the bike's rear seat handgrips and tapped Owen's good shoulder. "Fifth one in, on the left."

Owen rolled the motorbike slowly to the middle of the street and set down his foot. At the top of the driveway, lights lit up the first-floor windows of Officer Gessen's house.

Owen slapped up the helmet's visor. "You want me to come with you?"

She swung her leg over and slipped off her helmet. "No. I got this."

"You sure?"

She stood next to him, staring at the drive and the lighted windows. "I need to do this alone."

He nodded. "I've got your six."

She nodded. "Let's get him out here. Can you rev your engine?"

"Happy to."

The Triumph's engine roared for two beats then quieted. Owen flipped off the headlight and they were doused in shadows.

At the top of the house's walk, the front door opened and light poured across the sloped lawn.

Stewart Walker whispered, *Hello, again, Bob.*

Dom crossed the street and stood just beyond the reach of the pool of yellow.

Owen revved the Triumph again in one short blast.

Gessen moved slowly, tentatively down the walkway.

Dom thought of all the lies she and Beecher had told to keep the foster system at bay. She thought of the high school bullying about a disgraced cop who killed himself. She thought of the holidays she and Beecher had celebrated at their small table in the barren Brooklyn apartment. She thought of sitting among a sea of raucous families as she alone cheered Beecher across a graduation stage.

Gessen reached the bottom of the walkway and stopped.

This man took all that.

She breathed in to fill her lungs and slow her heart.

Gessen waited.

Her voice was strong, clear. "Velk tell you the Bureau is involved?"

Gessen squinted through the darkness at her.

She said, "The Bureau has eyes on you now. You and your goons."

His lips clamped shut.

"The wheels of justice turn slowly but exceedingly fine. They *do* grind."

In her ear, Stewart whispered, *It was always going to be you, my Dom, that finished this.*

Gessen scowled at her.

She said, "When they come for you—because they will come for you, I will see about that—I want you to know that it was Stewart Walker's daughter that nailed you."

Twenty minutes later, the Triumph thundered across the Verrazano-Narrows Bridge. Ahead, New York rose against a dark sky in all its glittering glory.

Exhilaration washed over her.

They'd done it. They'd cleared her father.

She flipped open the helmet's visor. Cold air rushed her face and adrenaline pumped her veins. She strained her neck and stretched her mouth open. Over the roar of the motorbike, she bellowed at the city.

She was free.

In front of her, Owen's helmet nodded vigorously.

She moved her hands around his body and clasped them tightly against his waist.

His right hand squeezed her forearm, held it close.

She leaned her helmet against his back and allowed a smile to break across her face. Speeding high above the churning waters of the Narrows with the glimmering city as a backdrop, it felt as if she were a bird flying through the night sky, soaring on air.

Chapter Fifty-One

KIEV, UKRAINE

The phone rang early in the morning. Out on the balcony, Ionna crushed her first and only cigarette and stepped inside through the window. She scooped up the pinging phone from the chair. "Officer Moroz."

"*Pani* Moroz. This is Zlata from Ludwig hospital."

Her mouth went dry. "Yes?"

"A few minutes ago, I had a call. From America. A young woman by the name of Lily. She is asking about a child born on December 28, 1996."

Ionna blinked. "Yes?"

"She left me her contact information. I am texting it through to you."

"Yes, Zlata, thank you."

"You will see that the information gets to the right people?"

"Of course."

"Good. Let us close this chapter so that the mother, the poor angel, so that her soul can rest."

Outside, a pigeon cooed.
Ionna said, "Yes. Let us do that."

Next in the FBI Agent Domini Walker Series

vinci-books.com/ofthunder

A missing boy. A hidden truth. A hunt that spans decades.

When Mila Pascale discovers a lead in her brother's long-cold disappearance, it points to a famous artist with something to hide. As FBI Agent Domini Walker digs deeper, she unearths a chilling conspiracy that won't stay buried.

Turn the page for a free preview

Echoes of Thunder: Prologue

Seven years ago

Mila Pascale's mother had been drunk for seventy-one hours. That was 4,260 minutes that her mother had been lying in the bed with the coffee mug of vodka. It had also been seventy-one hours since the police had first arrived.

Mila stood in the bedroom doorway. "It's about to officially be hour seventy-two."

Her mother squinted to focus. "What?"

"That will be 259,200 seconds." Mila liked the stability of numbers.

Her mother's forehead wrinkled.

"The FBI says the first seventy-two hours are the most critical." Mila's anger spiked and her heart thumped rashly. Exasperated, she rushed the words. "Seventy-two, Mother. Seventy-two. The FBI says that's the time to secure evidence, talk to witnesses. They say kidnappers hurt kids early. Seventy-four percent of stolen children are dead within three hours." She took a breath. Being the smartest in the family led to many frustrations. Many. She slowed her words. "That means their chances of them finding Jimmy are diminishing."

Her mother looked away. She didn't want to hear the numbers. She didn't want to hear a lot of things. Not now.

Mila stepped backward into the hallway.

She'd been the one to print out ten variations of Jimmy's photo. It was Mila who'd delivered them personally to the elementary school principal. It had also been Mila who'd shared a photo on numerous Facebook groups, including one for hobbyists who chased missing persons. Yesterday, she'd printed full-sized photos and stapled them on light posts across the neighborhood. Fourteen-year-olds could do a lot.

She turned toward Jimmy's room. The door was closed. Jimmy never closed his door. Ten-year-old boys didn't close doors. They wanted to be with the pack.

Walking slowly down the hall, she counted one foot in front of the other as she had since she and her brother had been little. Nine steps. Always nine. The permanent dimensions of the floor in relation to the variability of her growing legs meant that even if she shortened or lengthened her stride, it was still nine steps to Jimmy's room.

She stood in front of Jimmy's door and placed her palm against the wood. The characteristics of wood made it the same as the ambient temperature. Always room temperature. Unlike skin. Skin temperature changed depending on both internal and external factors. What temperature was Jimmy's skin right now? Was he running at top speed to escape someone, his skin bright red and burning? Was he bound tightly in thick wool? Or was he being held under frigid water?

She may never again know what Jimmy was feeling. Because according to FBI statistics, he wasn't ever coming home.

Echoes of the Thunder: Chapter One

Students filed into the large lecture hall of New York University's Waverly Building, dropped into seats, and pulled out laptops. On the stage, Professor Irawaddy stepped to the podium and set down his notes. He was a graceful, slight man with small shoulders and deeply black hair over a thin face. Even from the audience, his nose appeared long below wire-rimmed glasses. The fact that he never smiled added gravitas to his already very serious subjects. But his tone was always gentle and patient, as if he had raised many girls. Behind him, the large screen clicked to life.

Irawaddy was Mila Pascale's favorite professor. She appreciated individuals who were passionate about their specialty. This particular Criminal Justice Administration course had so far proven to be the foundational learning she had wanted for her career in the FBI. Over the last two months, Irawaddy had intertwined the dry issues of law enforcement management, policies, and procedures with exciting examples from the field. Last week, the title of his lecture had been "Technology in Use" and he had covered the work of the FBI's Operational Technology Division section that provided tech capabilities across the breadth of the Bureau's departments, from intelligence to national security. She had taken prodigious notes on their audio, video, and imaging support, including advanced electronic surveillance of wireless and data network communications. They also processed and collected counter-encryption and digital evidence. She imagined men in white lab coats breaking into computers.

Irawaddy clicked on the microphone and the students quieted.

The lecture title flashed on the screen. "Inter Agency Cooperation on Human Trafficking."

Like a fog bank, cold moved up through her chest.

His voice was raspy. "Since 2007, the National Human Trafficking Hotline has received over twenty-two thousand reports of sex trafficking cases. Of these, likely one in six missing and exploited children are endangered runaways. Globally, there are approximately 4.5 million people trapped in forced sexual exploitation. Roughly two million are children. It is a lucrative industry making an estimated ninety-nine billion dollars a year."

As if on its own accord, Mila's right hand reached down into her courier bag and clamped around a pen. There was no need for her to take notes on the laptop. She knew the stats.

The next slide was a graph detailing the demographic categories of missing children.

The fog slithered through her arms to her fingers. Holding the pen scissored between her index and middle finger, she twitched it back and forth in an even, staccato rhythm. Back, forth, back, forth.

As if from another room, Irawaddy's distant voice said, "In forty percent of stereotypical kidnappings, the child will be killed."

Back, forth, back, forth. She glanced to the left wall and focused on the brightness emanating from a wall sconce.

"We've seen that almost eighty-five percent of the perpetrators are male."

It had been 2,601 days since Jimmy had disappeared.

"Abducted children are predominantly female."

It wasn't healthy for her to count the days. But once she had started, it had been impossible to stop. It was just the way her brain worked. It hooked on to numbers, patterns, and rhythms. She had an obsessive personality and could get stuck on an idea or a goal. Before they had diagnosed her as being on the spectrum, a teacher had once described her as *stubborn like a pit bull*. Stubborn. Actually, she didn't mind the comparison to a pit bull because they were fearless and intentional. But her stubbornness wasn't a chosen character trait. Like being bossy. It was hardwired. Immutable. Her unique traits would also be an asset. Especially for the Bureau.

Irawaddy's voice was muffled. "Nearly half of all victims are sexually assaulted."

The thumping of her heart felt like a hammer trying to break her ribcage from the inside. The anxiety was swelling.

She set the pen down with a bang louder than she had intended. The neighboring student glanced over. Mila closed her eyes. *Breathe, breathe. Ten, nine, eight.*

An imaginary ghost brushed her wrist. Her mind stilled and her heart calmed as she welcomed the daydream and the illusory feel of Jimmy's hand on her arm. In the recurring memory, she was fourteen and walking Jimmy the four blocks to his school. He was talking about the show-and-tell session his class would have the next week.

His bright-blue eyes had been full of seriousness. "Lala, you need to help me." As a baby, he had mispronounced her name as "Lala" and it had stuck. "I really don't know what to bring."

She tried to smooth his cowlick the way Mother always did. "It's about showing the other kids something you really like."

Giving her a deep shrug, the bright yellow of his soccer shirt on his shoulders reached his ears. He pleaded, "Like what?"

"What do you like?"

His shoulders dropped emphatically. "Spaghetti and meatballs."

The logic was sound. He loved the past-due, discounted spaghetti and meatballs they purchased as takeout at the local deli. It felt as if they'd discovered a sneaky way to eat at a fancy restaurant. "That's not a bad idea."

He grinned widely.

"But, I mean, kinda all kids like spaghetti and meatballs."

He nodded sadly. "Sure. You're right. All kids love spaghetti and meatballs."

"What if you talk about something that's really valuable to you, something that others don't know much about?"

Up ahead at the corner, the crossing guard in a neon green vest was corralling a group of kids.

Jimmy said, "I mean, some of my Hot Wheels are really the best."

She gave him a questioning look.

He frowned. "All kids like Hot Wheels?"

"Don't they?"

"Yeah. I guess they do."

"I think you need something that is special to you."

He turned to her. "Lala, can I bring *you* into class?"

Jimmy was the nicest, kindest kid. She hugged his small shoulders and laughed. "Nope. Keep thinking."

She released his hand as they approached the waiting crowd.

He raised a finger. "I got it! The Rice Krispie treats that mix the sprinkles with the chocolate and white chocolate chips!"

It had been his own concoction. She nodded heavily. "That's a great idea. Very special. Very *Jimmy*. We can make it the night before. Ask Ms. Griffen today if you can bring that in and share with the class."

He punched the air with a fist and his wide smile showed off two big rabbit teeth. "Perfect! Thanks, Lala!"

The light changed and the bustling group of kids surged across the pedestrian walk.

He had given her a wave. "See ya later, alligator!"

From the stage, back in the present day, Irawaddy said, "Well, folks, that's all for today."

She took a deep breath to clear the tightness in her chest and felt the chilled fog dissipate from her veins.

He turned off the overhead screen and pushed down his glasses. "Please remember a few things as you get ready for the first exam in two weeks."

Around Mila, the class groaned. At the top of the laptop screen, a "new mail" icon began to blink. Most students turned off Wi-Fi in lectures to avoid distractions, but Mila knew her strengths and weaknesses: If she'd set a rule, she stuck by it. Her self-imposed structures were a source of pride. She may have been bad with people, but she was really good with rules. She ignored the blinking icon.

Irawaddy continued. "Remember to review the subjects going back to the first day. I will be putting in some questions on the administrative aspects, including budgeting, authorizations, and state and federal oversight."

The class groaned again. The neighboring student whispered, "Crap."

Irawaddy held up a hand. "I know, it's not glamorous, but you need to know who butters the bread of our agencies. That's a very important big-picture item." He rested his palms on the podium. "You can always connect with your teaching assistants if you have any questions. Have a good afternoon."

Around the hall, students snapped laptops closed and rustled through their backpacks.

Mila slid her fingertip across the finger pad and clicked open her inbox.

The sender was info@NCMEC.org and the subject line read, "We have an image for you."

Slamming through her veins like a tsunami, the fog bank returned.

NCMEC stood for the National Center for Missing and Exploited Children, the US clearinghouse for all things related to the prevention of and recovery of children. Every two years, the forensic artists would update a missing child's image to represent their best estimation of the child's current looks. Mila knew that so far, the Forensic Imaging Unit of NCMEC had done around 7,500 age progressions of long-term missing children. This had helped recover 1,800 children.

She blinked against the brightness of the laptop screen.

After the age of eighteen, MCMEC artists only did updates once every five years because at that point, a human face didn't change dramatically. Next year, Jimmy would be eighteen.

She closed the laptop and slid it in her bag.

On the top of a rounded hill in Washington Square Park, a Frisbee game had started. The outside city air smelled of fall's dry leaves. She fished out her phone from a jean pocket and texted Dom, *"Gonna stay in town, sleep @ apartment. Have early class."* It wasn't a lie. She did have an early class the next day.

Six months ago, two corrupt NYPD officers had stalked her Lower East Side apartment. Since escaping, she had been living with Domini and Beecher Walker just outside the city. The lease on the apartment wasn't up for another four months, so she'd been using it as a crash pad for long school days. Dom preferred her to stay in town if her schedule was tough. Dom replied, *"Sure."*

Mila shoved the phone back in the pocket. She did have an early class, but that wasn't why she wanted to stay overnight in the apartment.

She needed to be alone. To quietly view the NCMEC image. Maybe this was the year there would be a crack in the case. Maybe this was the year she found Jimmy.

Grab your copy…
vinci-books.com/ofthunder

About the Author

H.N. Wake spent two decades across Africa, Asia, and Europe, working first with the U.S. State Department and then with a global bank. Her expertise in human rights, democracy, and sustainability gave her a front-row seat to some of the world's most significant complexities.

In the early 2000s, Wake returned to the States to further her career. It was during those early mornings before the sun rose that she first attempted to write and, over time, discovered a powerful release for her demons.

Her books are marked by snappy dialogue, relatable characters, and razor-sharp research. Critics rave that her savvy, fast-paced thrillers resonate with a healthy dose of zeitgeist and feel as if they have been ripped straight from the headlines.

When she's not crafting edge-of-your-seat narratives, H.N. Wake is off traveling, sailing, or scuba diving—with many of her adventures sneaking into her plots. She currently calls the East Coast home, sharing life with her husband and their Tasmanian devil dog.

You can find her on a select few social media platforms.